To Kueser Kids!

John Combee

THE DRAGON STONE

a
pale horse
production

Library of Congress Control Number: 2001 130550
ISBN: 0-9710362-0-9

THE DRAGON STONE

RELATING
THE ADVENTURES AND NOBLE DEEDS
OF
CABAL,
KING ARTHUR'S DOG,
AS TOLD
BY
CABAL HIMSELF

*   *   *   *

TRANSLATED OUT OF THE
CANINE TONGUE
BY
MERLIN THE WIZARD

*   *   *   *

INSCRIBED BY ME,
BROTHER BLAISE,
ST. FRANCIS' FRIARY,
CRASTOR-UPON-SEA, NORTHUMBERLAND

part I

"I'm a lean dog,
a keen dog . . ."
— *Irene Rutherford McLeod*

I A Rude Awakening

S uddenly I was aware of the sound of tapping. Arthur had heard it too, for he was already trying to free himself from our tangled blankets. When he had, he gave the fur on my head a quick tousle. Then he crept softly to our chamber door.

"Who's there?" he said. "What do you want?"

"It's me, Emrys," came the familiar voice of one of the lads from the kennels. Arthur unbarred the door and opened it a crack. There stood Emrys, alone in the dark passageway. He held no candle or lamp. "We have to leave *now*," he whispered. "Merlin says there's not a moment to lose. Are you ready?"

Yes, we were ready—but we hadn't expected to be dragged out of bed in the middle of the night! Merlin had said first thing in the *morning*, and this certainly wasn't the morning! It was pitch-black outside, and I was still half-asleep. Arthur pulled on his boots and slung his knapsack over his shoulder. Then we set off after Emrys through the gloomy passageways of the Red Castle. The cold stones of those dark old stairways felt chilly against the pads of my paws.

We followed him down to one of the castle's postern gates. Merlin was there waiting for us and so was Arthur's brother Kei. Kei's dog Lupus—my own rough-and-tumble brother—was also there. Lupus and I sniffed noses by way of saying hello.

"All set, then, lads?" Merlin said in a half-whisper. Not waiting for a reply, he spun around and passed through the small doorway. He moved quickly down the steep path toward the River Wye, our sleepy-eyed band trailing behind him. A man was waiting for us with a boat to ferry us across the river. As soon as we were in, he began poling us across. No one said a word. Everyone seemed anxious.

The only sound was the lapping of the water against the boat. I lifted my nose, breathing in the strange river smells. I had no idea what this was all about, but from the way Merlin and Emrys were acting, I knew it was serious. I wondered if it had anything to do with the intruder who'd broken into Arthur's room last night.

When we reached the other side, we climbed out of the boat and clambered up the muddy bank. Merlin placed his hand on the barge man's shoulder and nodded his thanks. Then we set off along a path that angled away from the river.

The path took us beneath trees that bordered a meadow, and in a few minutes we reached a fork. One path branched off into the forest and the other went on around the meadow. Without hesitating, Merlin led us straight into the forest. There was a hint of morning in the eastern sky but we saw it only fleetingly, for we were soon deep within the forest gloom.

We traveled briskly for an hour or so, and my legs were just feeling weary when Merlin suddenly stopped. He whirled around and put his finger to his lips, and then he peered back down the trail. I was wondering what the old duffer was up to when I began to feel the vibrations. It only took a second to know what this meant—riders were on the trail behind us! I could just smell the scent of their horses and then I could smell the riders themselves.

I looked up at Merlin, cocking my head to one side and making a questioning little growl.

"Yes, Cabal, someone's coming. And I think we'd best get ourselves out of sight. I don't know who they are, but there are *some* folks out here we wouldn't want to meet."

Merlin hustled us off the path and into a terrible tangle of trees and bushes. We wriggled our way into the thicket and plopped down behind the protruding roots of an ancient beech tree.

"Absolute silence, lads," Merlin whispered. "They're almost here." Lupus and I lay flat on our bellies, our masters crouching beside us. The scents of the riders grew stronger. Then we could hear the clop clop clop of the horses' hooves. Peering through the leaves, I saw three men on horses nearing the spot where we'd left the trail. The one in front was studying the ground, and the others were looking all about. The hair on my neck started to rise, and I soon knew why— I'd begun to smell the scent of the very same fellow who'd tried to attack Arthur in our chamber last night!

Arthur, sensing my agitation, kept a firm grip on my collar. "Easy, Cabal," he whispered, "don't give us away."

Suddenly the riders stopped. The lead rider studied the ground carefully. He seemed puzzled.

"Something's fishy," we heard him say. "Up till now there's been clear traces of 'em, and now there isn't."

"They must've headed into the woods," said a second voice. "Must've heard us coming. Come on, let's go ferret them out."

"Yes," said the high-pitched voice of a third man, "let's go ferret them out!" And he gave a weird little cackle that I guess was a laugh. The other two started laughing also, as if the whole idea of "ferreting us out" gave them quite a bit of pleasure.

As I peered through the leaves, I saw each of them draw his sword. Then they turned their horses in our direction. And that's when Merlin started chanting a little sing-songy chant:

"Equibus phanticus, equibus stray.

Equibus franticus, equibus away!"

I glanced up at the old fellow in wonderment. What in blazes was he doing? His wizened old face was glowing brightly, and there was a strange gleam in his narrowed eyes. Merlin repeated his queer little chant three times—and then he got results!

The horses started nickering and rearing up, and their startled riders began shouting and cursing. And then, despite anything the men could do, the horses bolted. One of the riders smashed into an overhanging limb and crashed hard to the ground. The other horses charged off down the trail with their riders clinging to them for dear life. The third horse, now riderless, dashed off after them, abandoning the poor fellow who was writhing on the ground. Those horses were so frightened you'd've thought the Hounds of Hell were nipping at their heels!

"Let's *us* be moving too, lads," Merlin said, and he began shouldering his way out of the thicket. When he was clear, he set off at a run, the rest of us stringing out behind him. After we'd put some distance between ourselves and the path, our whole little troop settled into a steady jog-trot. We kept that up for a while, moving deeper and deeper into the forest. But at last the fresh energy our fear had given us was wearing off, and then it was all we could do to keep up with Merlin.

"Merlin!" Kei panted, his chest heaving, "we've been traveling for hours! How about we have a little *rest!*"

"Only a bit farther, master Kei," Merlin gasped back, "only a bit farther." The old geezer had a particular place in mind, I guess, and it wasn't long before we'd reached it.

It was a small forest clearing with a cluster of large rocks jutting up in the middle. That's where we were soon sprawled out, panting like anything, our tongues hanging out. Then Merlin and Emrys began digging around in their knapsacks, and lo and behold, out came some bread and cheese and dried fruit. Yumm!—Merlin! I shouted inside my head, I really love it when you make your magic! Lupus and I lapped up some water that burbled out of a little spring between the rocks. Then the whole lot of us got down to the serious business of munching.

"Hey, Merlin," Kei said, "would you mind telling us what in blazes has been going on around here? Who *were* those guys back there anyway, and what did they have against *us*? And what's the big idea of dragging us way out here in the forest?—a million miles from nowhere!"

"Oh, well, I shouldn't be worrying about *those* fellows," Merlin replied with a shrug. "That was probably just some little mix up."

"Yeah, right," Kei muttered, "just some little mix up! Those guys were going to *skewer* us!"

"As for what we're doing out here," Merlin went on, ignoring Kei's last remark, "you might say we're here for the sake of woodsmanship. Yes, master Kei, woodsmanship, that's precisely why we're here."

"*Woodsmanship*? You're telling me you've dragged Arthur and me all the way out here just to learn how to become foresters or something? *Really*, Merlin, *that's* rather beneath us!"

"Merlin," said Arthur, "is this the Forest of Dean?"

"Right you are, Arthur, that it is. And we'll be seeing a good bit more of it before we've reached our destination."

"And where would *that* be?" said Kei, "and what in blazes will we do when we get there?"

"Our destination, master Kei, is one of King Uther's hunting lodges. When you get there you'll be receiving some first-class instruction in the noble art of hunting. From Aled,

King Uther's chief forester. Your father's decided it's time you lads were spreading your wings a little. Now that your pups are a bit older and have mastered the rudiments of hunting, this seemed just the time for you lads to be having some real outdoor experiences."

I think everybody there knew that this *wasn't quite* the whole story. Something had been going on back at the Red Castle, something Merlin wanted to get us away from. This little trek into the forest was just an excuse to get us out of there. But one thing was for certain—if Merlin didn't want to talk about it, none of us would ever pry it out of him.

II Intruder in the Dark

The more I thought about it, the more certain I was that our flight into the Forest of Dean was connected to what'd happened to Arthur and me the night before.

That evening after all us young pups had been fed in the kennels, I'd been taken back to my master's chamber high up in east tower of the Red Castle. Arthur was there waiting for me, and the first thing he did was reach into his knapsack and pull out a cloth tied with a leather thong. Then he unwrapped for me my most favorite thing in the world—a juicy venison bone!

Arthur's little chamber had only one small window. An iron bar ran down the middle of it and there were two wooden shutters on the outside. Some evenings Arthur and I would sit there and look out the window at a river that moved in gentle twists and turns through a lovely green valley. Beyond the river we could see a meadow, and beyond that we could see nothing but forest.

Some nights Arthur would sit on a chest by the window and say things like, "Do you see how bright the stars are tonight, Cabal? Look up there, can you see Watling Street?" Then he would point to a bright band of stars spreading all across the sky. Or he'd say, "Cabal, do you see the moon's reflection on the water? The Wye looks pretty tonight, doesn't it?"

But Arthur always liked having a good night's sleep, and so did I. I was usually one very tired pup in the evenings, for old Tom kennelman and his helpers really put us through our paces. So after we'd had our fill of roughhousing, we'd snuggle up together in our blankets and go to sleep.

Now, my master Arthur has always been a very trusting soul. And up until that night he'd never even bothered to bar the door. People rarely came to our corner of the castle, and it never crossed our minds that anybody might try to harm us or mess with our things; besides, we didn't *have* many things. So every night at bedtime Arthur would snuff out the candles, pull in the shutters, and then we'd hit the hay. Well, we'd hit the rushes. But Arthur would always say, "Come on, old Cabal dog, it's time to hit the hay!"

Later that night, quite a while after Arthur and I had settled into our blankets, I was startled by the sound of our chamber door opening. Our door wasn't especially creaky, really, but I'd heard it just the same. And that's when I realized that someone *had just entered our room*!

I lay there listening. Yes, there was no doubt about it, someone *was* in our room! I could smell him and I could even hear him breathing. But why was he here? Had he brought a message for Arthur? Then why didn't he carry a lamp or a candle? And why didn't he call out to Arthur? And then he started moving across the room, creeping in our direction, stepping cautiously on the rushes—trying not to make a sound!

What in the heck was going *on*? Why didn't this person *say* something? Why was he moving so *quietly*? I really didn't like this—something was terribly wrong! Why would someone come sneaking around in Arthur's chamber in the middle of the night?

The shutters had been pulled together, but a little light came in around the iron bar. I slipped out from under our blankets and stood up, facing across the room. As the person was getting nearer, a growl began building in my throat. I tried to stop it but I couldn't—that growl just had to come out.

The person in the room had heard me. He stopped right where he was. He stood perfectly still—deciding what he should do, I guess. But I was getting madder by the second. *This room* was where Arthur and I lived! It was *our* place! This person shouldn't be *here*—not in the middle of the night, not when proper folks were asleep in their beds. No sir, I really wanted him out of here!

And then I began to bark. I just couldn't help it. Arthur didn't like me to bark, especially at night. But I just couldn't help it. I was *furious*, and I barked for all I was worth.

"Cabal!" Arthur called. "Whatever's the matter?" When Arthur spoke, that was when the intruder charged. He rushed right at us. And without hesitating, I rushed right at him, crashing against one of his legs. His knee bashed my shoulder and sent me flying. I must have surprised him, though, for as I went tumbling in one direction, he went sprawling in the other. I came down hard in the middle of the room, just as the intruder smashed against the wall.

When he hit the wall he let out a curse, and right at that moment something clattered onto the floor. Something shiny had slipped from his hand and fallen among the rushes. In a split second I'd pounced on it and snatched it up in my mouth. Then I dashed toward the window, where Arthur was throwing open the shutters.

Then, with the light of the pre-dawn coming in, we could see the back of a man lurching across the room toward the open door. He stumbled out the door and clattered down the passageway. I dashed after him and looked out, but by then he'd disappeared into the stairwell. I heard his boots clomping down the stairs, and then there was silence. Goodness me, was I ever glad to hear the last of *that* blighter!

Arthur blew on some coals in our fireplace and lit a candle. He took a good look around, but there wasn't much to see. Our few possessions remained untouched. I took a good sniff around, but that didn't yield much either. But there was one thing I knew for sure—if that fellow ever crossed *our* path again, I would know it and he would pay for it. For his foul-smelling smell was neatly tucked away deep inside the smell-cells of my little dog brain.

Arthur looked down and saw what I was holding in my mouth. "Peter, James, and John! Cabal, where'd that *dagger* come from? Is that what clanged on the floor? Stand still, boy—let's have a look."

Arthur carefully took the dagger from my mouth. Then he carried it over to the window and examined it. At last he looked back at me with a serious, worried look. Then he dropped down beside me and hugged me all over.

"Good old Cabal," he said. "I'm sure glad you didn't get hurt! Can't have my brave old hunter getting hurt."

Arthur patted me some more and smiled anxiously. Of course I'd always known that Arthur loved me. But right then I could tell that Arthur didn't just love me—Arthur *really* loved me! And *that* made me feel like I was ten feet tall!

Afterwards, Arthur and I sat there in the early morning light with the candle still flickering in the middle of the room. A lot of the time I can tell what Arthur is feeling, and right then I knew he was terribly puzzled. I reached up and nuzzled at his hand. Arthur smiled at me and tousled the fur on my head. At last he got up and went over to the door. He glanced down the empty passageway and then swung the door closed. For the first time since I'd been with him, Arthur placed a great bar of oak across the inside of the door. "That'll take care of uninvited guests," he said. Then we settled down once more among our blankets.

As we lay there, Arthur snuggled up and whispered in my ear, "You know what I think, you silly old fur-dog? I think someone just tried to *kill* me. And you know what else? I think you just saved my life. Cabal," he said in all seriousness, "I am very much in your debt."

Goodness, Arthur, I thought to myself, you aren't in my debt! *Any* self-respecting dog would have done the same for its master. And I knew in my heart that Arthur would never hesitate to do the same for me.

Arthur seemed lost in his thoughts. "*Why?*" he said at last, with an anxious look on his face. "Why would someone want to hurt *me*? Do you have any idea, Cabal, because I surely haven't?"

Well, I certainly *didn't*! If Arthur didn't know what was going on, how could you expect *me* to know? I'm just a dog, after all, and a young one at that.

III *Taliesin the Bard*

We traveled that day through the Forest of Dean until late afternoon, when Merlin brought our little troop to a halt. We were still a good ways from our destination, he said, so we were going to have to spend the night in the forest. He led us to an open spot beside a small stream, and while he and Emrys got busy with preparations for supper, Kei and Arthur went off in search of firewood. For the first time that day, Lupus and I were left to our own devices. We were soon sniffing all around, checking the place out good.

Close by the stream stood a tall clump of grass with an oddly pungent fragrance. Lured by the smell, I went over and sampled a few blades. Seeing what I was doing, Lupus came over and took a few chews also—then he stopped abruptly and shot me a very disgusted look. Looking all huffy, he went over and took a big pee against a tree stump, and then he turned his back on me. I guess my brother and I had different ideas about what tasted good.

Kei was filling a large cooking pot when he spotted me munching on the grass. Then he let out a big whoop of laughter. "Hey Arthur, come take a look at your weird dog! What a brute you are, Cabal! Cabal's a grass-eater, Arthur! Oh, beware of mighty Cabal, the fearless eater of grass!"

Arthur put down the firewood he'd been collecting and came over to pat me.

"I'd appreciate it if you wouldn't refer to my dog as a brute, Kei. Cabal is no brute! He's a gracious, gentle beast with a highly refined palate. Mock him if you must, Kei, but this noble canine isn't ashamed of his liking for salads. Maybe your rugged old Lupus needs to dine on fillet of dragon or rack of ogre. Well, that's quite all right, Kei. You can have your rugged old Lupus. Give me my gentle Cabal. I wouldn't trade him for any dog in the world—not now, not ever."

In response to Arthur's little speech, Kei said something rude which I think I'd better not repeat.

A little while later, when we'd gathered around the campfire and were about to plunge into our evening meal, a voice called out to us from the forest.

"Hello there! I say, would you be willing to share a bit of your fragrant repast with a wandering minstrel who's both hungry and weary?"

"Come forth and show yourself," replied Merlin with caution in his voice, his hand sliding down onto the hilt of his sword.

A slim young man stepped out from the trees and slowly approached our fire. He appeared to have no weapons other than a knife that hung from a strap across his chest. On his back was a large and lumpy pack. He came up close to the fire to warm himself, and as he stood there, he looked us over good. We looked him over good right back, and I *sniffed* him over good, too, but I didn't find any whiff of danger about the young fellow.

"Do you travel alone?" asked Merlin.

"I do," he replied. "And I'd be much in your debt if I could share your fireside this night—and perhaps if you could spare it, a bowl of that savory soup whose smell has enticed me."

"Enticed you, has it?" said Merlin. "Well, sit you down then, and when you've supped, you can repay us in song. For if I'm not mistaken, you're the one they call Taliesin the Bard."

The stranger grinned at Merlin. "My reputation has preceded me. But let me assure you, if your soup tastes as good as it smells, I'd be delighted to sing for my supper."

"How 'bout he sings for his supper *after* supper," said Kei. "I'm starvingly hungry, you know!"

"My sentiments exactly," said Merlin. "I'm starvingly hungry too. Tuck in, everyone, and let the devil take the hindmost."

We didn't waste any time in reaching for the food, and the young stranger wasn't far behind us. As soon as he'd set down his pack, he pulled a wooden bowl and spoon from an inner pouch and joined us by the fire. In a moment he was matching us slurp for slurp and munch for munch.

After we'd eaten enough to take the edge off our hunger, the boys couldn't contain their curiosity any longer.

"Are you truly a wandering bard?" asked Arthur with awe. "Have you sung at the courts of dukes and earls and kings? Can you sing about Hector of Troy, or Jason and the Golden Fleece?"

"Where are you heading now?" asked Kei. "You could travel with us, if you'd like! Or you could stay at our father's castle! It's not far from here. It's called the Red Castle."

In just about no time flat this Mr. Taliesin the Bard was being treated like a famous celebrity! Well, not by me! I was going to reserve *my* judgment until I'd heard him sing. He *looked* okay and *smelled* okay, but what was that funny-looking thing in his pack, anyway? And what kind of singing voice could this skinny young fellow possess?

After everyone had had their fill of soup and bread and cheese, we were all feeling fine and dandy, sitting there beside the warm fire on a cool dry summer's night. Then Taliesin opened his pack and took out a wooden thing with rows of strings all across it. It turned out to be a thing called a harp. As he plucked at it and fiddled with it, I pricked up my ears and cocked my head in astonishment at the strange sounds. Then, in a high melodious voice, Taliesin began to sing.

"You have heard, no doubt, of the wondrous treasures,
Of the thirteen treasures of Britain.
Those treasures of old, with their powers untold,
By which many a man has been smitten."

Taliesin sang about a whole bunch of strange things—a cauldron of plenty, a cloak of invisibility, a flaming sword, and some other things like that. When he finished, we all wanted to know more about the thirteen treasures of Britain.

Kei, who really loves horses, wanted to know all about the Bridle of Rhiannon. If you put it on your horse, no other horse could run fast enough to catch you. Arthur was fascinated by a magical set of chess pieces—when you put them on the chessboard, they became tiny living people. Then they played a game of chess all by themselves, and during the game they yelled rude things at each other, just like warriors in a real battle! Merlin's ears really perked up at the mention of something called the Dragon Stone, a precious gemstone that only could be possessed by the person destined to become king. But for me the most interesting thing by far was the Cauldron of Plenty. Anything you wanted to eat you could get from it, anything at all! I could just imagine all the mouth-watering venison bones I would get from that wonderful cauldron!

Then Taliesin sang about a boy called Alexander who'd been able to ride a great black stallion that nobody else could ride. Arthur and Kei really liked that one, and I did too, for it was a lot more exciting than the one about the thirteen treasures. Then Arthur asked Taliesin if he knew any songs about more recent events.

That's when Kei blurted out, "Oh, Arthur, who cares anything about *that*! Come on, Taliesin, sing us one about *sex*!"

Everybody laughed at that, including Merlin. Taliesin said he'd just been working on a song that happened to concern fairly recent events *and* sex. Then he began to sing about a place in Cornwall called Tintagel. He sang about the Duke

of Cornwall and his wife Igraine, and about King Uther
Pendragon, the High King of Britain. The High King had
started a war against the Duke because he'd fallen in love
with the Duke's wife. The Duke, not surprisingly, hadn't been
happy about that. I can't remember all of it, but here's how it
started out.

Love was the lure that drew lonely King Uther,
Love for the lady who lingered long in Lyonesse.
Her charms had enchanted the High King of Britain
And caused him to come to the wild craggy cliffs,
Where the tides tossed and tumbled at far-off Tintagel.

Now the doughty Duke of Cornwall defended just two
    castles,
High-towered Tintagel and many-turreted Terrabil;
And the Duke's dwindling divisions—decent men all—
Fought firmly and fiercely, caused their foemen to fall,
As the tides tossed and tumbled beneath lofty
    Tintagel."

The despot grew desperate, despairing of the lady;
He summoned his seneschal, his sage advice sought.
Then a message to Merlin his messenger bore swiftly,
To the wizard whose wonders must be worked for the
    king,
As waves crashed wildly on the cliffs at Tintagel.

Then came Merlin the Magus in mysterious ways
    moving;
Dark deeds he would do there to achieve the king's

desire,
But a price must be paid him, a precious prize be
    given:
His choice was the child whom the Duchess would
    conceive,
While waves wearing white-caps washed rocky
    Tintagel.

Remarkable magic was made there by Merlin,
Who transformed in a trice the King's trusty advisor;
He lent him the likeness of the Cornish lord's
    liegeman,
Then did the same for himself in just a few seconds—
As the tides tossed and tumbled beneath towering
    Tintagel."

The last thing this Merlin fellow did (was he talking about *our* Merlin, I wondered?) was make King Uther look exactly like the Duke of Cornwall! Then the three of them walked right into Tintagel Castle, and no one even suspected they weren't who they were pretending to be! Those foolish, foolish folks at Tintagel, I thought! Didn't they have any *dogs*! If they did, those dogs of theirs were a terrible disgrace to dogdom!

Anyway, Uther Pendragon got what he wanted— which was to spend the night with the Lady Igraine. And Merlin got what he wanted—the child that was conceived that night. The only one who didn't get what he wanted was the Duke of Cornwall, for that poor bloke got killed. Later on the little baby boy, the son of King Uther and the Lady Igraine, was taken away, and no one knew what had become of him.

Taliesin's song created quite a stir, and when he was finished, the boys bombarded him with questions. Taliesin admitted that he wasn't a real expert about all of this—he'd pieced his song together from odds and ends he'd heard. Besides, he'd only been a boy when these things had happened. But Taliesin said there might be someone else close by who knew more about it than he did. "If anybody really knows what happened at Tintagel," he said, "it would have to be Merlin."

The boys looked expectantly at their old teacher. But stoney-faced Merlin just sat there quietly, lost in his thoughts. A strange hush settled down on us then as we waited for Merlin to say something. Finally, he did.

"Well, lads, I suppose I do know a few things about those events of nearly fourteen years ago. In those days I was well acquainted with the folks in Taliesin's song—especially Uther. Yes, I knew the man fairly well. Maybe *too* well, in fact. But speaking of King Uther, it's just possible that you lads will be meeting the man yourselves in the not-so-distant future."

Well, *that* caused quite a stir! The boys wanted to know what Merlin meant and how he knew this. But at that point the old geezer decided to clam up. And once Merlin was clammed up, we knew that's how he would stay.

After that Taliesin played a couple of songs that everyone knew. Kei and Arthur and Emrys joined in on the choruses, and even old Merlin began croaking out a few of the words sort of under his breath. Then Lupus took it into his head to join in too, and I'm sorry to say that kind of brought the party to an end. I actually thought he was sounding pretty good, but no one else seemed to share my opinion.

Then we all settled down for the night. Arthur pulled a thick warm blanket over us, and Arthur and me, well, we hit the hay.

IV   Kei Brings Home the Bacon

At first glance King Uther's hunting lodge in the Forest of Dean wasn't at all impressive—why, it wasn't a bit like being at the Red Castle! It was just a ramshackle old place that'd definitely seen better days. But once we got settled in there, it actually turned out to be rather cozy. A couple named Aled and Branwen lived there; it was their job was to kept the place ready in case King Uther turned up to do some hunting. Let me tell you, those folks did an excellent job of keeping that place stocked with tasty things to eat!

As we stepped through the door, incredible aromas greeted our noses. Somehow, Aled and Branwen must've known we were coming, for dinner was ready and waiting. And believe me, we were ready and waiting for it! Later that night, with our bellies full of bread and stew and our legs achingly tired from our long tramp through the woods, we dragged ourselves up a set of wooden stairs and flopped down on the hay-covered floor of a loft. That's when I finally found out what Arthur meant when he said it was time to hit the hay. Kei and Arthur spread out some blankets over the hay, and then the four of us hit it. And I'm happy to say, it didn't hit us back.

I awoke the next morning to the sound of rain gently thrumming on the roof. Even though I was still sore all over, it felt good just to lie there listening to that soothing sound. That's when I began to smell a delicious aroma wafting up from below. "Peter, James, and John!" said Arthur. "What's that *fantastic* smell?" My master's nose, it was clear to see, was working also.

"It's chestnut-flower biscuits, lads," came Merlin's voice from below. "But if you want any, you'd best hurry." With Lupus and Kei right on our heels, Arthur and I clattered down the rickety stairs and dashed to the kitchen. Seated on stools around a broad plank table, and chewing contentedly, were Branwen, Aled, Emrys, and Merlin. "Well, thanks for waiting for us!" I barked grumpily. Fortunately, another tray of freshly-baked biscuits was cooling on the hearth.

My word, did those flaky little cakes ever taste good! They were brown and crispy on the outside, white and doughy on the inside. With a dab of melted butter and a dollop of sweet honey, it's hard to imagine anything tasting better— well, I guess I'd make an exception for venison bones.

All that day the rain pattered down. The boys spent most of it with Aled, who showed them various kinds of spears and javelins, different styles of bows and arrows, and other stuff people use for hunting.

Merlin stayed in the kitchen chatting with Branwen as she busied herself with baking and cooking. They were exchanging a lot of gossip, mostly about people I'd never heard of. And then when the subject turned to cooking recipes, why, it was *Merlin* who turned out to be the big expert! I've probably told you that I've never met another man quite like Merlin. Believe me, I haven't.

When we woke up the next day, Merlin was gone. That was Merlin—here one day, gone the next. He didn't come back until four days later. In the meantime, the weather had turned dry and warm, and that meant we had a forest to learn about.

On that first day of good weather, Arthur and Kei went off into the woods with Aled. As the the king's forester, it was Aled's job to guard the forest and make sure no one hunted without the king's permission. If they did, it was a kind of stealing called poaching. Believe me, you don't want to know what happened to someone who got caught poaching!

Aled fitted the boys out with bows and arrows and instructed them in their proper use. Then Arthur and Kei spent the whole afternoon practicing. From what I heard that evening, it turned out that Arthur was the better shot—which really irked Kei! We only heard about this, though, because Lupus and I hadn't been with them. Emrys had taken us off to a different part of the forest and worked with us on identifying animal smells.

I'd soon come to realize that there are actually *two* forests—one that's cared for and one that's left completely alone. The one that's cared for is a pleasant place, with huge oaks and beech trees, gentle streams, and even a few small farms scattered here and there in forest clearings. The untended forest, though, is dark, dense, and menacing. The only folks who live there are outlaws—folks who'd kill you just as soon as look at you. But to tell you the truth, that was the part of the forest that fascinated me the most. And on our fourth day at the hunting lodge, events occurred that took us deep into the untended forest.

Here's what happened. That afternoon we were all out in the forest together when Lupus began barking and leaping around like some kind of maniac dog. Then he went rushing off into the untended part of the forest, with all of us chasing after him. We followed him quite a ways until we'd reached a very deep and dense section of the forest—a place that stank to high heaven! It didn't take long to figure out that Lupus had discovered a pig run, a special track used by wild boar.

Up till then the only thing I knew about any boar was that its bones were tasty, crunchy, and long lasting. But Lupus and I were about to learn that the wild boar is the most dangerous creature in the forest. Strong, quick, and fearless, he has razor-sharp tusks that can slash you and gash you quicker than you can say Joseph of Arimathea. Not only is he completely fearless, he's also as vicious as they come!

Aled and Emrys put their heads together and considered the situation. Aled certainly wasn't eager to be messing about with any boar. But at last they decided that we would go ahead and see if there really was a boar on the pig run today. From the way Lupus and I were dancing and prancing, they had to know that the scent was pretty fresh. They also had to know the risks that were involved. But I guess they decided it would be good for the boys to have a little taste of some real danger. It turned out that that was *not* such a wise decision!

The men and boys were each carrying a short spear, which was one of the most effective weapons to use against a boar. And Aled and Emyrs also had good sharp swords. It appeared, at least, that we were properly equipped for dealing with a boar, if one should really turn up.

Aled and Arthur crouched down among the bushes on one side of the pig run, and Emrys and Kei hid on the other. Lupus and I were couched beneath a nearby tree. Being "couched," as Lupus and I both knew by then, means to lie quietly with your nose between your forepaws, ready to dash after your prey upon receiving your master's signal.

And that's when I got my first real whiff of boar! Goodness gracious me, what an ungodly smell! Whew! That boar smelled *ripe*! Sometimes when I haven't had a good cleaning in a while Arthur says that I smell ripe. But that boar smelled riper than any animal I'd ever had a whiff of. I usually like powerful smells. But *this* one was too powerful even for me!

Now I knew the boar was getting really close, for I could actually feel him coming! I could feel the drum-beat of his feet as he rushed along. And then *there he was!*—a huge dark shape hurtling down the trail! Aled stepped out into the path in front of him, his spear held low, but the boar kept right on charging. And just as Aled was thrusting his spear upward, that's when the boar *swerved*—straight at Arthur!

Arthur jabbed at him, but his spear glanced off the boar's muscular chest. By then the boar was jerking his head back and forth, back and forth, his terrible tusks flashing wickedly. Arthur cried out in pain. Then the air was filled with the smell of blood.

Emrys' spear came flying in from the other side of the trail. It sank deep into the boar's flank, quivering like an arrow in a target. The boar grunted and danced backward a few steps, but his eyes were still fixed on Arthur. That stinking swine meant to finish the job he'd already begun.

Just at that moment Kei was readying *his* spear. Quickly he raised his arm above his head, pausing for just a second in the cocked position. Then he whipped his arm forward in a smooth and graceful motion. The spear knifed through the air and caught that terrible monster right in the throat. Kei's spear sank deep into the boar's flesh—and then boar blood was spurting like anything!

But the boar's final lunge had already been set in motion, and wounded though he was, he hurled himself forward. He crashed down hard on top of Arthur, who crumpled beneath the weight of the boar. In the next moment, Aled had reached the tangle of bodies. He jerked the boar off of Arthur and plunged his sword deep into the monster's chest. At that point there was nothing more to say except, "So long, Mr. Boar! May you *rot in hell forever!*"

Just for good measure, Lupus and I rushed over to that terrible brute and tore at him with our teeth. That didn't do much good, of course, since that vile smelling creature was already a goner; but at least it let us feel that we'd been a part of things too. Phew, what a stench! Good riddance, I thought, to a pile of stinking, rotten rubbish!

And then I remembered Arthur. Oh my goodness, what had happened to Arthur? There he was, lying on the ground with Aled and Emrys and Kei hovering over him. Blood was everywhere. I tried to get to Arthur, but Emrys grabbed my collar and held me back.

Aled rolled up his coat and placed it under Arthur's head. Then Arthur opened his eyes. Doing his best to squeeze out a smile, Arthur said, "That smelly bugger didn't much like me, did he, Aled! I've sure become unpopular lately! First someone comes after me in my room—and now even the beasts of the field have turned against me!"

I slipped out of Emrys' grasp and wriggled my way to Arthur. I licked his face good. The blood on Arthur was mostly the boar's, thank goodness, though not all of it; for that horrid monster had made a pair of deep gashes right across Arthur's chest. He'd made a terrible hash of Arthur's shirt, but much worse were the two little furrows his wicked tusks had plowed right through my master's flesh! Arthur said he would be fine, but I knew those wounds must've hurt like anything.

Aled cut away the tattered remains of Arthur's bloody shirt. Then he laid strips of cloth over the wounds and bound them tight. That would have to do, he said, until they could be dealt with more properly back at the hunting lodge.

Kei and Emrys lifted the body of that stinking boar onto their spears to take it back with us. Then we started back through the forest toward the old hunting lodge. Our little troop moved slowly, yet everyone seemed very much on edge—by what had happened, I guess, and by what had *almost* happened!

Lupus and I were so keyed up it was all we could do to keep from dashing off after squirrels. And the people were just as keyed up, especially Kei. He kept describing the whole thing over and over, and every time he told it his spear toss got more wonderful than the time before. Pretty soon Kei's prattle was getting on everyone's nerves. Finally Aled snapped at him, "Give it a *rest*, lad! Just give it a *rest*!"

Poor Kei seemed stunned by Aled's sharp rebuke. But leave it to my master to stand up for his obnoxious brother.

"It's all right if you need to talk about it, Kei. We don't mind a bit—at least, I don't. After all, you really saved my hide today! And believe me, that's something I won't ever forget!"

At last we straggled into the old hunting lodge, with a live Arthur and a dead boar. And who should be sitting happily by the fire clutching a mug of ale but Merlin. When he learned that Arthur had been injured, he got about as worked up as I've ever seen him. The old geezer seemed really anxious until he'd determined for himself that Arthur's wounds weren't so serious as they might've been. That evening Merlin was as gentle and loving toward Arthur as I'd ever seen. And that was when it dawned on me that I'm not the only one who really loves Arthur. Merlin loves him a lot too—maybe *almost* as much as I do!

V   *A Royal Visit*

and a Royal Pain

It was wonderful to be home again, back in the Red Castle and back in the little room that belongs to just Arthur and me. I was so excited that I rushed all around, sniffing at all the things we'd left behind on that cold morning a week ago. *A week ago?* You mean it was only a week ago that Emrys had come rapping on our door at that unholy hour of the morning? My word, it seemed a lot longer ago than that!

There, lying in the corner of the room, was Arthur's old sleeping pallet, looking very bedraggled. And there was our little fireplace, with a neat stack of wood all laid out in case we wanted a cheery fire. And there was our window, where we could look out over the River Wye. And there, far off through our window, was the forest—the forest I used to wonder about, the forest I now knew quite a bit about.

Kei and Arthur were excited to see their parents, and the words came tumbling out of them. I stood there listening as they poured forth the story of our adventures. And as I did, I realized something. In the time we'd been gone, Kei and Arthur had changed. They still looked pretty much like the same boys, and yet somehow I knew that they weren't going to be boys for very much longer. They were boys who had begun to outgrow their boyhood.

After a few days the excitement of being home again died down and life returned to normal. Kei and Arthur spent a lot of time on their studies with Merlin, and when they weren't doing that, they concentrated on their riding. Both of them loved horses, and they'd always spent their extra time hanging about the castle stables. Now they went there every day, perfecting their skills.

Lupus and I returned to our training with the other young dogs. Now Emrys and Tom kennelman were teaching us about hunting horns, what their sounds meant, and what we should do when we heard them. I caught on quicker to all this than the others did, which earned me a goodly amount of praise. You know what? I didn't mind a bit.

Then late one afternoon, just after we'd come in from training, we were startled by the sound of riders. In through the castle's great gateway clattered three sudden-appearing riders, and what an impressive sight! As their horses pranced across the cobblestone courtyard, the riders' capes billowed out behind them, and sparks shot out from the horses' hooves.

The arrival of this trio of knights caused quite a commotion, for we soon learned they were messengers sent from King Uther Pendragon! They'd come to inform us that the king and his royal party would be arriving here tomorrow. *Here*, at the Red Castle, *tomorrow*!

King Uther's messengers cut dashing figures. They were all decked out in their knightly finery, with plumed helmets and shiny armor, and their shields had colorful designs on them. They were the handsomest fellows we'd ever laid eyes on. A crowd gathered in the castle courtyard, and I heard people whispering their names. One was called Sir Griflet, and the others were Sir Lucan and Sir Bedivere. Sir Lucan and Sir Bedivere were brothers, and they looked a lot alike— sort of the way Lupus and I look a lot alike.

That evening the trio of knights dined in the great hall with Sir Ector and the Lady Olwen, along with Merlin, Kei, and Arthur. Lupus and I were there too, for by then we were treated like full-fledged members of Sir Ector's household. I listened in on everything that was said that night, which was mostly about the High King and his visit. Queen Igraine was coming too, and for some reason that I can't explain, that made me very excited. The King's advisors were coming also—Sir Brastias, the King's marshal, Sir Ulfin, the King's chamberlain, and Sir Jordan, the Queen's chamberlain. Of course I didn't know what marshals or chamberlains were, but it sure sounded grand.

But there was one thing about this that had me baffled. In all their talk about the royal visit, no one said one word about the *reason* for the visit. Sir Ector and the Lady Olwen didn't even ask. Surely they were as curious about that as I was? Kei and Arthur didn't ask either, but those two lads were in such awe of the knights, I'm sure they wouldn't have said anything that ran the least risk of being rude.

It seemed strange to me that no one mentioned the reason for the visit. It isn't as if Sir Ector is one of King

Uther's most important nobles or anything. And while the Red Castle is a nice enough place, it's certainly not famous. In fact, as I've heard Arthur say, we lived pretty much off the beaten track. Why, then, were we being honored with a royal visit? I was definitely flummoxed.

You should have seen all the activity the next morning! The castle was being spruced up like nothing I'd ever seen. Everybody was working their backsides off, including Arthur and me. Our usual lessons had been called off, and Kei and Arthur had been given lots of little tasks. I wanted to stick close to Arthur, but I also wanted to steer clear of all the folks scurrying about doing this, that, and the other.

A little before noon Arthur and I found ourselves heading for the stables. Arthur was making sure all the stalls were ready for the horses of the royal party. This was a big responsibility since they'd be bringing a lot of horses. In fact, some of Sir Ector's horses had been moved to temporary quarters outside the castle just to make room for them.

As I may have told you, Sir Ector's stables was one of my favorite places. I was on good terms with most of the horses there, especially a lovely roan named Ajax and a huge chestnut named Brutus. They were Sir Ector's two best horses. Most of the horses in the stables were pretty good-natured, and I liked being around them. But with horses you always have to be careful. They're large and powerful animals, and just like anybody else, sometimes they get cantankerous.

The stalls were clean and tidy, and Arthur congratulated the stable lads on their work. He told them that if they took good care of the king's horses, the king might take good care of *them*. Their eyes certainly lit up at *that*! My eyes lit up when Arthur said it was time for us to find ourselves some lunch.

High atop the tallest tower in the Red Castle, Arthur and I sat all alone, munching on apples and bread ends as the readying of the castle continued below us. A long double-pointed banner, Sir Ector's finest pennon, flew proudly above our heads, snapping in the breeze. It was silver and red like the banner that hung on the wall in the great hall. It was just the thing to greet the High King's eyes as he approached the Red Castle.

By late in the day everything was ready, and everyone there was terribly excited. Earlier in the afternoon Sir Griflet, Sir Lucan, and Sir Bedivere had ridden off to meet the royal party and lead them here. And now a man was shouting down from high up on the tower where Arthur and I had had our lunch that the King and his royal entourage were approaching the castle. At last they were almost here!

And in just a few more minutes, there they were, riding through the gateway of Sir Ector's castle, two by two. First came Sir Bedivere and Sir Lucan, then Sir Griflet and a knight I didn't know, and then several pairs of riders who turned out to be the King's advisors. Then came the King himself, the High King of Britain, King Uther Pendragon, and beside him rode none other than *Merlin*! Now, how in blazes did Merlin get there, I thought, scratching my head? Following the King and Merlin came Queen Igraine, with one of her attendants riding beside her.

My goodness, was she ever lovely! I'd never seen such a beautiful, elegant lady. But there was something *else* about her that really startled me; for the more I looked at her, the more familiar she seemed. But how could that be? How could this beautiful lady on whom I'd never laid eyes look so familiar to me? I didn't know what to think. Again I was flummoxed.

Sir Ector helped the Queen dismount from her horse. And then everyone in the castle went down on their knees to the King and the Queen. It was really something to behold! And then all sorts of things were happening—people were being guided places, things were being unloaded, and horses were being led off to the stables.

Because Arthur and I were responsible for the care of the royal horses, we went along with the grooms and stable boys to see that everything was going smoothly at the stables. My word, those horses were getting the royal treatment! Relieved to see that everything was under control, Arthur praised the stable boys, and then he and I started to leave. And that's when disaster struck.

Just as I was passing an open stall, out of nowhere I was whammed by a thunderbolt. I sailed through the air and smacked up hard against a wall. But smacking the wall was the least of my problems, for it seemed as though one whole side of my body had been crushed in. I gasped for air but I couldn't *get* any! I really thought I would suffocate right then and there and *die*.

Then I heard Arthur shouting. And then as I lay there, crumpled in the dust and the straw on the stable floor, it slowly dawned on me what had happened. I had been the victim of a vicious attack. I had been the target of a monstrous creature's malice. I, Cabal, the gentle grass-eating dog, had been bashed in the ribs by one of the horses we'd been treating so royally. Now *there's* gratitude for you!

VI The Dragon Stone

All I remember of the next few hours is pain, excruciating, unrelenting pain. Then I realized that I was back in Arthur's room, lying on our old sleeping pallet, the poor old pallet I'd been so rough on when I'd been a pup. But the most important thing was that Arthur was with me. At some point Merlin had come, for I remember him rubbing something on my side and that I didn't hurt quite so much when he was finished. Arthur stayed by me the whole time, rubbing my head and chest and talking softly. He looked very sad-faced. I felt almost as sorry for him as I did for myself.

I don't know how long things stayed like that. I dozed off for a bit, though it was a funny kind of sleep. Then I heard a knocking on the door. Arthur went to see who it was. It was Emrys, come to tell Arthur that the banquet for the King and Queen was about to begin.

Arthur shook his head sadly. "Tell them I'm sorry," he said softly, "but I won't be coming. Tell them I can't leave Cabal. I hope they'll understand."

Emrys just stood there, looking as if he didn't quite believe what Arthur was saying—that Arthur was turning down the chance to dine with the High King and Queen of

Britain, the chance of a lifetime. Finally Emrys shrugged and set off down the passageway to deliver Arthur's message.

A few minutes later there was another knock on the door. This time it was Kei.

"Come on, Arthur!" he snapped. "Dinner's about to start! *We've* got seats at the *high table*, right beside the King and Queen. Even Sir Lucan and Sir Bedivere don't get to sit at the high table. So, come on! Give that grass-eating dog of yours a hug, and let's go! We're already late!"

But Arthur wouldn't budge. He told Kei that he couldn't possibly leave me—not even if the Pope himself had come to dinner. I didn't really get that last remark, but I was glad Arthur wasn't going to desert me. My side was hurting like anything, and the last thing I wanted was to suffer alone. I wanted somebody else to suffer with me—and Arthur was the one I wanted.

A few minutes later there came yet another knock on the door. "What *is* this!" I thought crankily. "Can't you people just leave us alone?" It's a good thing I can't talk, because this time it was Sir Ector who'd come to speak with Arthur. As far as I could remember, this was the first time he'd ever come to Arthur's room. Goodness, I thought, this must be important to him.

Sir Ector looked very anxious, but he took a moment to come over to me and pat my head. "Good old Cabal," he said, smiling down at me. "Merlin says you'll back in action in a few days. I hope so. We can't get along around here without your help."

Then Sir Ector turned to Arthur. "I understand your feelings, Arthur, and I respect you for having them. But this evening's dinner is about the most important thing that's ever happened to us, and the King and Queen will be greatly disappointed if they can't see you tonight. They wanted to meet you and Kei and get to know you. They have some things they want to discuss with you, Arthur, things that will be important to you. Emrys can stay with Cabal, if you'd like. But please, Arthur, for my sake and your own, come down and have dinner with the royal party."

I could tell that Arthur was really squirming. He wanted to be at this special dinner as much as anything, and I'm sure he didn't want to disappoint Sir Ector or do anything that might offend the King and Queen. If I could've talked, I would've told him to go ahead. I could survive a few hours without him—if I *had* to.

Poor Arthur was really torn. At last he just shook his head. "I can't come, father. I want to, I truly do. But I can't leave Cabal. Cabal needs me."

Sir Ector looked at Arthur for a moment, not saying anything. Then he patted my master on the shoulder and gave him a loving smile. "You're a loyal person, Arthur, and Cabal is lucky to have such a friend. That quality will serve you well when you've become a knight." Then Sir Ector turned away and went out of the room.

We sat there quietly, just Arthur and me, both of us feeling a lot of pain and a good deal of sadness. Then Arthur busied himself with starting a fire because a damp chill had crept into the room. The fire helped to make things a little cheerier, but a feeling of gloominess remained over us. I'd begun to feel guilty that I'd kept Arthur from being at Sir Ector's dinner, and I think Arthur was feeling terrible that he'd gone against his father's wishes. This was probably the first time Arthur had done something other than what his father wanted him to do.

After a while there came another knock on the door. It was one of the lads from the kitchen bringing Arthur a tray of food. I guess if Arthur wasn't going to come down to dinner, dinner was going to come up to him. That was something, at least. But neither Arthur nor I had a whole lot of appetite at that point. It's hard to eat when you're feeling sad and blue, or in my case, sad and *bruised* and blue. Arthur finally managed to get down a few bites, and then he placed the tray on the floor beside me. I managed to get down a few bites too. But mostly, Arthur and I just looked at each other with sad, gloomy eyes.

Then I heard the sounds of more footsteps outside in the passageway, and then there came yet another knocking on the door. I was beginning to lose count of how many visitors Arthur had had today—it was a record, I have no doubt of that. The door opened and there was Merlin; behind him stood Emrys holding a pair of stools. Behind Emrys were some other folks that I couldn't quite see.

"Arthur," said Merlin, "you have some visitors who would like to sit with you for a while. I hope you and Cabal will make them welcome." Emrys stepped quickly into the room and placed the stools close to the fire, and then he and Merlin went out again. And then in came King Uther Pendragon and Queen Igraine.

"Good evening, Arthur," said the Queen, in a soft gentle voice. The King nodded silently to Arthur and walked straight across the room to me. He bent down beside me and began to stroke the back of my neck. As he did, I got a big whiff of the King's strange smell. That smell made me very uncomfortable; it was the smell of someone who was terribly sick.

Then the King took a look at my battered side. Thank goodness he knew enough to just look and not touch. I sensed that he was a man who knew quite a bit about dogs. And I knew right then that he was a man who'd loved a dog or two of his own.

"So this is the one who's kept you away from us this evening," he said to Arthur. "He must be a very special dog. Either that," he said with a tight little smile, "or you have no great interest in kingly things."

Arthur seemed to be struck dumb. He stared wide-eyed at the King and Queen. Finally he had the presence of mind to bow down on one knee and say, "Your Royal Highnesses, I am *truly honored*."

"Come and sit by us, Arthur," said the Queen. And she picked up Arthur's stool and set it by the fire beside the other two stools. Then all three of them sat by the fire and looked shyly at each other in silence.

King Uther Pendragon, I said to myself, the High King of Britain, right here with Arthur and me in our plain little room, way off in a remote corner of Britain. Who would ever have imagined it! And Queen Igraine, once so beautiful that men had fought a war over her—and still the most beautiful woman *I'd* ever seen!—the woman Taliesin had sung about that night in the forest. Here they were, right here with Arthur and me in our plain little room. Here were Uther and Igraine and Arthur, sitting side by side on three small wooden stools, right here in our room. Goodness, I thought, will wonders never cease.

I studied the King and Queen as they sat there beside my master. They were wonderfully impressive people in their looks and bearing. Uther, I thought, looked like an old, worn-out hawk. His eyes were piercing and his long curving nose was as sharp as the beak of a falcon. But the man looked tired and weary, and hovering over him was the smell of sickness. This man, I thought to myself, is dying.

Igraine, though no longer young, looked younger than King Uther and seemed in much better health. And although there was a touch of silver in her light-brown hair, her eyes were clear and sparkling. But as I looked at her, I just couldn't get over the feeling that I'd seen her before, even though I knew that was completely impossible.

And then it came to me. As they sat there together by the fireside, Uther and Arthur and Igraine, I realized why I felt I'd seen the Queen before—it was because in her eyes and across her forehead Queen Igraine looked exactly like Arthur. What in the world, I thought, what in the world?

It soon became clear that Igraine was the one who would have to get the conversation going—if there was going to be any conversation—because Uther, like Arthur, was definitely not the talkative type. A man of action rather than words, I supposed. Anyway, Uther seemed content just to sit there and look at Arthur; and Arthur, not the liveliest of talkers at the best of times, was much too shy to do a lot of talking in the presence of the King and Queen.

"Arthur," said the Queen, "Merlin has told us a great deal about you. Did you know that Uther and I have been following your progress for quite some time now? Merlin has been singing your praises to us for several years. He's quite fond of you, Arthur, but I imagine you know that. He tells us it won't be long before you and Kei have earned places for yourselves among Britain's finest knights. We have been eager to meet you, for it's young men such as you who will soon be called upon to help Britain face her uncertain future."

Then Igraine began to ask Arthur many questions, mostly about the things he'd been studying with Merlin and about his training in weapons and horsemanship. She wasn't kidding when she said they'd been following Arthur's activities, for she knew more about what Arthur had been doing than I do—and I *live* here!

"Arthur," said the King, finally joining the conversation, "I imagine you'd like to know why we're here." (Aha, I thought, our liege lord has finally gotten around to the sixty-four shilling question!) "We've come to ask a favor. We want you and Kei to come up to London next spring as soon as the weather allows for safe travel. We believe there's a time of great trouble ahead for Britain. We want our finest young men to come together and prepare for the storm that's gathering over the land."

"My liege," Arthur said softly, "what troubles are these that lie ahead for Britain?"

King Uther remained silent a few moments before grimly replying, "Invasion from without; and almost certainly, rebellion from within. Much of it has to do with me, Arthur," he said with a sigh. "You see, our mutual friend Merlin tells me that the days remaining to me are now very few. And as you probably know, that old devil is usually right. If I could only live just a few more years, Arthur," the King mused sadly, "perhaps the future wouldn't look so bleak."

The King was studying Arthur's face closely. "What's your age now, Arthur? Fourteen?"

"I'll be fourteen next May, my lord. Kei is fourteen now, and he'll be fifteen this coming March."

"I just wish I had more time," Uther mused. "If only I had a few more years, it might make all the difference."

The Queen placed her hand gently on Uther's arm and smiled at him. "Perhaps you'll have more time than you think, my dear. It's never possible to be certain about these things. Even Merlin isn't always right."

"No, only ninety-nine times out of a hundred. But in any case, Arthur, you must come to London in the spring. It appears you may have to grow up a little quicker than you would have done under other circumstances.

"Now," said Uther, reaching inside his cloak and bringing out a small wooden box, "I have a little gift for you. It's something quite special, and you must guard it very carefully. Whatever you do, *don't lose it*. And don't show it to anyone except Merlin. And be sure to bring it with you when you come to London. Before long you'll understand its true significance."

Uther handed the box to Arthur, who cradled it gently in his cupped hands. I lifted up my head, ignoring the pain, in order to get a clearer look at what was going on. It looked like a plain ordinary little box. Then Arthur removed the wooden lid. There, on a small piece of dark red cloth, lay a brooch. I think it was a shoulder pin for a cloak. It glittered in the light from the fireplace. It was oblong-shaped and made of silver. There was an intricate design worked into the silver all around the outer edge, and set into the middle of the brooch was a fierce-looking dragon. The dragon's body was formed in red gold. Its eye was a huge red gemstone that gleamed and sparkled in the firelight. In stunned silence, Arthur stared at the beautiful object in his hands.

That really is quite a gift, I thought, a truly kingly gift. But it seemed to me that if they'd come here for the purpose of handing out gifts, they really should have brought a little something for everyone—wouldn't you say?

Just as I was thinking those rather petty thoughts, Queen Igraine reached into her handbag and took out a small leather pouch. She loosened the draw strings and pulled a piece of dark red cloth from within the pouch. She carefully unwrapped the cloth, and there before my eyes appeared a juicy, meaty bone—venison, my favorite!

"Do you think that Cabal might feel up to dealing with this, Arthur?" she said. Arthur nodded, a big grin on his face.

"My lady," I thought to myself, "I don't mean any disrespect, but that's what I'd call a silly question." As a matter of fact, I did feel up to dealing with the Queen's gift. And it wasn't long before I'd done just that.

part II

"Let dogs delight to bark and bite,
For God hath made them so."
— *Isaac Watts*

I Troubles Galore

Arthur and Kei didn't go to London that next spring, and they didn't go to London the following year, either. It was nearly two years before they went, and what terrible years they were.

Now, I'm going to tell you a little about those years, and you may find yourself wondering how in the world a simple country dog like me could know so much about events happening all over Britain. But before you start getting skeptical, give me a chance to explain.

You've probably heard the expression "walls have ears," right? Believe me, walls *do* have ears, especially in a place like the Red Castle. Folks have to be careful what they say and where they say it, for you never know who might be listening in. But *dogs* have ears too, and yet people say all sorts of things around us, never imagining that we're listening. Believe me, we *are*. And that's how I know what I'm going to tell you—by listening. It really pays to be a good listener.

Arthur and Kei didn't go to London that spring because they no longer had a reason to go. Merlin had been right about King Uther's health, and Uther had been right about the troubles that lay ahead for Britain. When the King had visited us at the Red Castle, he'd known that he was dying.

But he'd expected to live another year or two, and maybe even longer than that if he was lucky. But Uther wasn't lucky, he was downright *un*lucky.

A few weeks after the New Year had come and gone, a messenger arrived bringing word that the High King was dead. We were saddened by this terrible news, and we mourned the passing of our King. But not everyone in Britain felt the way we did. In fact, while we were mourning, others were preparing for war!

Uther Pendragon had died without having an heir, and he'd died before announcing to the people of Britain who he wanted to succeed him. He had planned to do that at the great Easter gathering of Britain's finest nobles. Now everything had changed. Now the rulership of the kingdom was up for grabs—and plenty of folks were out there grabbing.

Chief among them were three of the lesser kings. King Lot of Lothian was one of them, and he had a powerful army to back him up. King Uriens of the Land of Gore was another, and he had the remarkable skills—some said the *magical* skills—of his wife Morgan le Fay to back him up. I'd actually seen those two fellows one time when they'd made a quick stopover at the Red Castle. That was right about the same time that we went off on our excursion into the Forest of Dean.

The third fellow who was out there grabbing was called King Nentres of Garlot. I'd never heard of him before, but now we were hearing quite a lot about him, and it appeared that he was every bit as crafty as the others. Merlin said that

King Nentres was as likely to emerge from this whole business with the crown perched firmly on his head as anyone.

Oddly enough, the three lesser kings were married to sisters, a troublesome threesome called the Cornwall Sisters— Morgan, Margaux, and Mergit. They were the daughters of Igraine and her first husband, the Duke of Cornwall, who'd been killed in a war with King Uther. I remembered hearing Taliesin sing about all that. These three women had great ambitions for their husbands; and they also had great ambitions for themselves.

And to make matters worse, now bands of pagan Saxons had begun plundering the villages along the southeast coast of Britain. In some places they'd even been making settlements. Britain needed a powerful army to send them packing, but until there was a High King, no one wanted to deal with the matter. On top of that, every little tuppenny thief and robber in the kingdom had decided that this was the perfect time to emerge from the holes they'd been hiding in. Now traveling had become extremely dangerous, and folks only went out on the roads if they absolutely had to. When they did, they traveled in large groups.

What times these were! People weren't safe anywhere, not even in their own homes. And that included us. Even in our snug little castle with its high walls and towers, tucked way off in the west of Britain, even we weren't safe.

Early one spring day about a year after we'd learned of the king's death, Merlin came swooping into the Red Castle without a bit of notice. Then he went swooping right out again—with Kei and Arthur in tow! It was quite a sight to see old Merlin come charging into the castle that day mounted on a gigantic black horse. In only a moment's time he'd fetched the two boys and was calling for swift horses.

Just before they left, Merlin sent Arthur scurrying back to our chamber to collect a few last things. When Arthur got back Merlin whispered, "Do you have it?" When Arthur nodded his head to say "yes," Merlin seemed very relieved. Then he hustled the boys onto their mounts, and the three of them went dashing off. Kei was on Brutus and Arthur on Ajax, the fastest horses in Sir Ector's stables. They went on their way without taking a single dog to protect them! And Merlin, drat him, didn't even give the boys time to say a proper goodbye. In the blink of an eye, Arthur was gone. It was six long and lonely months before I saw him again.

A few minutes later a large raiding party came charging up to the Red Castle. Without even asking, they barged right in! Sir Ector was furious, but he didn't try to stop them. He let those raiders search the castle from top to bottom and bottom to top. They peeked and poked everywhere. But when they didn't find what they were looking for, they went tearing off to look someplace else.

I really didn't know what were they looking for. Merlin, I suppose, or maybe Kei and Arthur. I kept a close watch on them as they ransacked Arthur's poor little room. It infuriated me to see them putting their grubby paws all over our things. At one point their leader rushed in and shouted,

"Well, haven't you *found* it yet! Come on, you worthless so-and-sos, *find it!*"

Then one of the fellows he was shouting at held up a small box he'd fished out of Arthur's chest. It looked familiar to me and I was trying to remember when I'd seen it. The leader tore off the lid and felt inside. Discovering it was empty, he hurled it against the wall, smashing it to bits. "Come on," he snarled, "let's get out of this stink hole!"

At last they'd gone! Unfortunately, now their smelly smells were all over our stuff! And as I sniffed around our room, I suddenly realized that one of those smells was the scent of that knife-wielding no-gooder, the fellow who'd snuck into our chamber one night. The time is going to come, I promised myself, when I'll get my little paddy-paws on that fellow—and then we'll see how much he enjoys *that*!

Arthur's long absence was nearly the death of me. I was so sad, all I did was mope. I didn't feel like hunting, or chasing cats, or hardly even like eating bones. Lupus was sad too, and we spent a lot of time just lying around, curled up together, licking each other. Emrys knew something had to be done about us, and he knew just what to do. He took us down to the kennels, and from then on he never let us go back to our masters' rooms. He kept us with the other dogs and made us do everything they did. He was keeping our minds occupied, and it was a good thing he was.

For the next six months Lupus and I lived full, active lives in that world of dogs in Tom kennelman's kennels.

There's a lot I could tell you about it if you really wanted to know. But it doesn't concern Arthur, so I'm going to skip it. I'll only say that Lupus and I did fine in the kennels, earning our places and earning the respect of Tom and Emrys. And then, just as suddenly as that phase of our lives had begun, it came to an end.

It was early evening on a crisp fall day. Tom and his helpers were bringing us back from the fields where they'd been working us. We all came trotting over the drawbridge and into the Red Castle, a weary but happy pack of dogs, when all of a sudden it hit me. While we'd been out, something at the castle had changed. I couldn't quite put my paw on it, but I knew something was different. After we'd eaten supper, I *really* knew something was different, because Emrys came into the kennel and took Lupus and me away from the others. He led us across the open courtyard toward the castle's great hall, a place we hadn't set paw in in a mighty long time.

But before we got there, I knew what had happened. I knew it because my nose had picked up a scent I hadn't sniffed in a very long time—it was my master's scent! Arthur, my nose was telling me, had come home! Arthur, my nose was shouting at me, was right here, *right here* in the Red Castle! Lupus began dancing, and I knew he'd picked up Kei's scent. Why shouldn't he be dancing? He was one excited fella, and so was his brother Cabal. Believe me, Cabal, the gentle grass-eating dog, was one excited fella.

Lupus and I charged toward the entrance to the great hall, and there they were—Kei and Arthur! We were all over them in a flash, and they were all over us. Yes, it was Arthur, it really, truly was. It was a somewhat different Arthur, a bigger, taller, older Arthur, but there was no doubt that it was my own dear Arthur. This person who was hugging the daylights out of me had the wonderful smell that could only belong to Arthur; this person who I was licking the daylights out of had the gentle, loving touch that could only belong to Arthur.

II On The Road—

The London Road

That fall turned out to be the last one that Arthur and I would ever spend at the Red Castle. It was a fall in which a lot of things happened. Late in September, after the Feast of St. Michael, Sir Ector received some exciting news. As a result of that news, we were going to London! And we wouldn't be waiting until spring. We were going to London before Christmas.

Let me tell you why. It was because a fellow called the Archbishop of Canterbury and a fellow called the Bishop of London had persuaded the lesser kings to come to London to determine, once and for all, who would be Britain's new High King. And believe it or not, all those guys who'd been wrangling over the kingship had actually agreed to this. So now all of Britain's nobles would be gathering in London at Christmas time.

The key figure in all of this was Bishop Baldwin, the Bishop of London. He'd had a special kind of dream called a *vision*. He'd been told in his vision that during the Christmas season the Lord Himself would reveal the identity of the new

High King of Britain! Goodness me! I wondered if such a thing could really be possible?

The second exciting thing that fall was that Kei had become a knight. This occurred in November at the Feast of Allhallows. Now he was no longer plain old ordinary Kei, now he was "Sir Kei, knight of the realm." Next year it would be Arthur's turn to be knighted; but during our trip to London he would serve as Sir Ector and Sir Kei's squire, and Emrys would serve as their yeoman.

By early December, preparations were well underway for our journey to London. Needless to say, we were a very excited bunch. But for Arthur and me the most exciting thing of all was the wonderful new horse Merlin had brought to the castle.

Merlin hadn't been around much since Arthur and Kei had come back home from Northumberland—in case you'd been wondering, that's where he'd taken them when he'd whisked them away from the Red Castle. They'd been staying at a friary with a man named Blaise. He was an ancient holy man who a long time ago had actually been *Merlin's* teacher!

Anyway, in his usual fashion Merlin suddenly turned up one day, and with him was this incredible horse, a sleek, young, high-spirited mare. From the look of her, I was guessing she'd be able to give Brutus a pretty good run for his money—and in case you don't know it, Brutus is a mighty fast horse! But the best part of all was that she was going to be *Arthur's* horse.

Kei was really irked when Merlin said the mare was for Arthur. For once, it seemed, Kei's younger brother was going to get something better than what Kei had. Kei had known for a long time that his father would give him Brutus just as soon as he became a knight, and he was always bragging about what a great horse Brutus was. But then when Merlin shows up with an even better horse—and it was for *Arthur*!—believe me, Kei was pretty peeved! Well, that was just too darn bad, because *that* was how it was going to be!

Arthur wasted no time in getting to know his new horse. He worked with her several hours a day, and after a few days he'd decided to name her Tawnyfoot. That was because one of her forelegs was a lighter shade of brown than the others. She was an independent critter, that's for sure. But Arthur has always been good at winning folks over—animals included—and it wasn't long before Tawnyfoot was eating right out of his hand. And what I'd first suspected about her turned out to be true—she was one of the fastest horses anybody at the Red Castle had ever seen. As old Tom kennelman might say, "that girl could move like the autumn wind."

On a bleak December morning we set off for London. Sir Ector, riding Ajax, led us on our way on. Kei rode behind him on Brutus, and Arthur followed on the high-stepping Tawnyfoot. Emrys rode a sturdy Welsh pony named Cinder, and behind him, perched on a gray, came Davi, the old fellow who looked after our pack horses.

That afternoon we were joined by two other small groups from the nearby castles of Grosmont and Skenfrith. Now we'd become twelve in all—seven older men, three younger men, and two loyal, courageous dogs. Among those who'd joined us was a lad called Hervey. He was Kei's age, and like Kei, he'd recently been knighted. Sir Rhys, Hervey's father, was one of Sir Ector's best friends. Hervey and Kei already knew each other, and right away they were acting like the very best of pals. Arthur, I could tell, felt a little left out. But he always had *me*—his loyal, loving dog.

The narrow, crooked roads we followed sometimes took us through small villages. Folks wary of passing strangers peeked out at us from behind their shuttered windows. Their dogs, though, didn't hesitate to rush out and bark their fool heads off. Lupus and I acted tough, letting those local dogs know that if they wanted a tussle we were ready for them. They rarely did, which was a relief, since we didn't really want to fight with them.

Towards evening on our second day we reached the city of Gloucester—my word, what a place! I'd never imagined a town could be so big; and it was completely surrounded by high walls. People could only get in through a huge gateway with massive doors and a huge iron grid called a portcullis. Once we'd entered the city, there before us were more buildings than I had ever seen. There was one gigantic one that loomed way up high in the darkening sky. Arthur said it was the minster. It was some kind of church, I guess,

but what a church! Its towers rose higher than the towers at
the Red Castle.

Sir Ector led us to a street that was packed with inns
and hostelries. It was packed with people, too, who crowded
around fires or huddled in doorways or just milled about. None
of the places could fit us all in, so we divided up and found
rooms where we could. The room we found was at a sad-
looking place called The Nag's Head. The sign out front
showed a pitiful-looking horse with a long scrawny neck, eyes
that bugged out, and a mouth full of huge yellow teeth!

Our room was pretty pitiful also—cramped and smelly.
All it contained was a rickety bench and three moldy straw
mats—home, no doubt, to more crawly things than we wanted
to know about. But at least we had a place where we could
get ourselves a decent night's rest. Unfortunately, getting a
decent night's rest wasn't what Kei and Hervey had in mind.

III   Styx, Stones,
and a Broken Bone

Hervey and Kei led us through the streets of Gloucester in search of supper. The smells that emanated from the inns we passed seemed plenty inviting to me. The boys, it seemed, were being rather choosy, but finally they found one that was to their liking. The sign out front had a picture of a ferryboat taking some folks across a wide river.

"The River Styx," said Kei with a laugh. "*This* looks like the place for us. Shall we, my dear Hervey?"

"Yes, let's," replied Hervey with a grin.

Through the partly open door came laughter and some other sounds faintly resembling singing. Kei and Hervey pushed their way in. Arthur went in after them, and so did Lupus and I.

"Good evening, my dear Cerberus," said a bleary-eyed fellow as I entered the room. "Your heads, my dear Cerberus, are looking quite splendid this evening."

My *heads*? What did he mean by that? I only had *one* head as far as *I* knew. I've met some pretty strange birds in my time, but this fellow was right up there. His comment about my heads had me worried for a moment. But he had more to be worried about than I did, for when someone bumped against him, the poor bloke fell backwards and landed right on *his* head! He lay there completely still, out cold on the cold stone floor. A pair of serving lads dragged him away, and that was the last I saw of my strange welcomer.

By then Kei and Hervey had elbowed their way through the throng to a table at the far end of the room. Arthur was working his way more cautiously, and as he edged past one of the serving girls, I saw her reach over with her free hand and give him a little squeeze on the arm.

"Make yourself comfy, love," she said, giving him a wink. "I'll be with ya 'fore ya know it."

"Oh, uh, thanks," Arthur said, giving her an embarrassed little grin. Then he looked around hurriedly for Kei and Hervey.

In contrast to the nippy air outside, the atmosphere inside "The River Styx" was warm and nostril-filling. Maybe it was even a little *too* rich with the odors of folk's bodies, but there were other smells there that were definitely to my liking, in particular the delicious fragrances of food. Also to my liking was the sight of a roaring fire blazing away in a huge fireplace. Iron spits were being turned by red-faced boys, and hunks of meat were sizzling and dripping their juices onto the coals below. Umm, the sight of all that meat started my mouth to watering.

Kei and Hervey called out for a pitcher of the hot mulled wine that everyone was drinking, and one of the serving girls soon obliged. A moment later she was back with a basket of freshly-baked bread and a platter loaded with pickled onions and chunks of a pungent-smelling cheese.

In no time at all the boys were attacking the bread and cheese, Hervey using an ivory-handled dagger that he wore on his belt, and Kei making good use of a single-edged hunting knife he'd been given by Aled, King Uther's forester. Arthur pulled out his own pride and joy, the very knife I'd knocked loose from an intruder one night, back when I was still a foolish young pup.

Hervey kept sploshing the spiced wine into wooden cups, and he and Kei kept glugging it down. That was their chief interest at the moment, whereas Arthur kept glancing in the direction of the serving girl who'd touched his arm. After a while she came over to talk to Arthur. She started joking with him and teasing him as if she'd known him for years. Arthur was having trouble figuring out what to say to her, but I could tell he liked the attention.

From across the room someone yelled "Jill!" in a very loud voice. The girl glanced nervously toward the voice. Then she asked us seriously if we needed anything else. Now you're talking, I thought, for Lupus and I had needs that went far beyond bread and cheese—needs that included the luscious meat that was spending too much time turning over the fire and not enough time churning in our bellies. Arthur told her exactly what we needed, and he also asked her if she could find any bones in the kitchen. She gave him a toothy grin and said she'd see what she could do, for "the urgent needs of such a fine young lord shouldn't go unattended."

Lupus and I chewed on crusts of bread while we waited for the good stuff to arrive. While we waited, I glanced about the room, trying to get a better idea of this place that Hervey and Kei had dragged us into.

Close to the fire sat a cheerful group that must've already enjoyed quite a lot of the spiced wine. They were red-faced and happy and making a heart-felt effort to sing Christmas carols—but I had a lot of trouble understanding their words. At another table a dice game was in progress, and these fellows were taking their activities very seriously. There'd be a moment of intense silence while all eyes were on the guy who was rolling the dice; then after he rolled, there'd be cheering from some and cursing from others. At one point a man leaped up from the table, snatched off his cloak and boots, and flung them at another man who caught them against his chest with a great burst of laughter. The first guy looked really angry.

"That poor chap seems to've lost his shirt," said Hervey a little too loudly. His remark brought a whoop of laughter from Kei, which brought all of us a very dirty look from the fellow who'd lost his cloak and boots.

"Hey, come on," Arthur said to Kei and Hervey. "Keep it down! Or we'll be buying ourselves a bushel of trouble." But Kei and Hervey, who by now had had quite a few cups of the wine, didn't seem especially worried about that.

At last the serving girl who'd been flirting with Arthur turned up with our food, at which point Lupus and I settled in under the table, applying ourselves with gusto to a platter of truly gorgeous bones. I'm afraid I was rather preoccupied for a time and didn't pay much attention to what was going on. But after a bit, when I finally came up for air, I realized that the atmosphere in the room had changed.

Many of the people who'd been in the room earlier were gone now, including the carolers who'd been sitting by the fire. The dice game was over too, and several of the men who'd been in it were just now crossing the room toward our table. The man with no boots was one of them, and he looked madder than ever.

He came right up to us and stood by our table, looking daggers at Kei and Hervey and Arthur. For some reason, especially at Arthur. Then he raised a big meaty fist and shook it right in Arthur's face.

"You keep away from my Jill, boy. Don't you *touch* her or *talk* to her or even *look* at her!"

By the end of this his voice had become high and quavery. Then he banged his fist down on the table, causing the empty wine pitcher to tumble onto the floor where it shattered—too darn close to my head for comfort!

When I looked up again I could tell that Arthur was thinking fast, trying to decide what to say to this drunken bozo. Knowing Arthur the way I do, I knew the last thing he wanted was to get into a brawl with this brute and his rough-looking associates, who were now positioned all around our table.

If Arthur had had a chance to speak, maybe everything would have turned out differently. Unfortunately, before Arthur could come up with just the right words, it was Kei who had to go and open his big mouth.

"Why my dear *sir*," he said sarcastically, "of course we won't look at your sweet little Jill. Of *course* we won't talk to your lovely little Jill. And *heaven forbid* that we should lay our hands on her tender young flesh! (Who'd want to anyway, right Hervey?) But can *we* help it if your little Jill wishes to do those things to *us*?"

When Kei's words had finally sunk in, that angry behemoth reached out and grabbed Kei by the shirt, jerking him up off the bench. With his face right up against Kei's he spit out a final warning.

"If you sissies ain't out o' here in the next five seconds, *blood's gonna be spilt!*"

"*Do your worst!*" Kei shouted back. He shoved the man's chest with both hands as hard as he could, which sent the pair of them sprawling onto the hard stone floor.

The man with no boots landed smack on his back, and Kei came down heavily on top of him, knocking the wind right out of him. In a flash one of the man's companions leaped onto Kei's back, which brought Hervey leaping onto that man's back. In no time at all the man's friends had joined the fray, and then of course Arthur and Lupus and I did likewise.

What happened in the next few minutes is all kind of a blur. Bodies were tumbling and crashing everywhere, legs and arms were thrashing and lashing. People were shouting and cursing and groaning. Lupus and I danced and dodged amongst the tumbling bodies, employing our teeth to best advantage. Lupus got one of the best opportunities, biting some poor bloke right in the middle of his flabby backside. I sure hoped that fellow wasn't planning to take any long horse rides any time soon!

The innkeeper kept running up and down, yelling at us to stop! stop! stop! "You're *wrecking my place!*" he screamed at the top of his lungs. "You're *wrecking my place!*" He was right about that! When he realized his yelling and

threatening were getting him nowhere, he ran out into the street, calling for help. Amazingly, he got it.

Into the room rushed three tall men. Right away they began grabbing the fighters—who were pretty exhausted by now, anyway—and pulling them apart. Lupus and I hid out under a broken table and watched as these fellows soon put an end to the fighting. Then Kei looked up and gasped, "Sir Bedivere? Is that *you*, Sir Bedivere?"

Now that you mention it, it really *was* Sir Bedivere! And Sir Lucan and Sir Griflet! Now what in the world were *they* doing here? While I was reflecting on this curious business, I heard a terrible groan from behind me. I glanced around to see Hervey lying on the floor, holding one arm pressed against his chest. Arthur heard him too and was soon stooping over him, seeing what he could do.

The fight was over now. The bootless man and his friends had disappeared, leaving the place to us, the three knights, and the woebegone innkeeper. That poor man looked around with tears in his eyes, surveying the damage and rubbing his hand back and forth on the side of his face. He sure looked pitiful. But when Sir Bedivere pulled a gold coin out of his pouch and placed it in the man's hand, boy, the innkeeper brightened up in a hurry.

When we surveyed our own damage, it was clear that Kei and Arthur had received their fair share of bumps and bruises. But it was Hervey who'd gotten the worst of the deal. He had a deep gash across the side of his face, but his real agony was caused by the arm he clutched against his body. Sir Lucan checked Hervey over good, then shook his head.

"The cut shouldn't be a problem," he said, "but as for the arm, well, it looks like it's broken."

The three knights walked back to the Nag's Head with us. Then Lucan took Hervey off someplace to have his arm attended to. It took us quite a while to calm down again after all the excitement. But finally Kei, Arthur, Lupus, and Cabal (known to some as Cerberus), called it a night.

IV   *London Town*

We came into the City of London through a marvelous gateway that Sir Rhys called Aldersgate. It was the city's main entrance from the west, and it was *gigantic*! Yet big as it was, it wasn't big enough for all the people and wagons and animals that were trying to jostle their way through. Fortunately, most of these folks were going into the city rather than out, which allowed us to be carried along with the tide.

An hour earlier I'd begun to smell smoke from the city's fires. Then I'd begun to see a gray haze hanging motionless in the sky. Then, when we were closer, we could actually see the high walls of the city rising up before us. Now here we were, smack in the middle of that heaving throng, pushing our way through Aldersgate and into the city of London.

Once we were through, we moved down a main thoroughfare toward the heart of the city. And as we did, the sights and sounds and smells of that amazing place came rushing over me—especially the *smells*. There were so many of them that I didn't even try to sort them out, I just let them wash over me in a symphony of fragrances, in a rhapsody of aromas. They were delicious and mysterious and inviting, and some were even a little frightening. And I wasn't the only one who was overwhelmed by London, for Arthur and Kei were gazing all about like a pair of big-eyed pups!

People were engaged in every kind of activity, and what a racket they were making. Outside of shops men and women were shouting, urging people to come inside and buy whatever they were selling. Wagon drivers yelled at folks to get the heck out of their way, and some of those folks made rude remarks right back. Sometimes their rude remarks were accompanied by the shaking of fists, or other gestures, and once I even saw a couple of men *swinging* their fists! But most of the folks just ignored such commotions and went on about their business. After a few days, when we'd become seasoned veterans of city life ourselves, we could ignore all the distractions; but on that first day us lads from the country hadn't yet developed that knack. So we moved on into the city feeling a little dazed and a lot amazed.

Sir Ector had taken rooms for us at a place called The Mermaid, a large inn on Candlewick Street. We had two rooms on the first floor above the street; Sir Ector and Davi would be in one, and Kei and Arthur and Emrys would be in the other. I was soon giving our room the once-over, while Arthur, as he so often did, was gazing out the window.

"Cabal! Look over there! That's the *Tower of London*!" Arthur pointed off to the left at a massive castle that rose above the other buildings close beside the River Thames. "Cabal, look over *there*! That's the Church of St. Paul—*St. Paul's Cathedral*!" Now Arthur was pointing off to the right toward a huge church we could only see a part of. It rose way up above the rooftops of the city. But Arthur, I wanted to say, come over here and take a look out the *back* window! Don'tcha see all those cats lolling about by the stables, looking for all the world like they could use some stirring up? How about we take a little stroll out there this evening?

After a bit Sir Ector took the boys off in search of food. Lupus got to tag along, lucky dog; it was my turn to stay behind and keep an eye on our belongings. I sniffed around the room some more and then settled down in our blankets for a little dognap.

I was startled into wakefulness by the sound of someone climbing through the back window. "What the heck is *this*!" I thought, growling fiercely. I rushed over to investigate, only to discover that the intruder who was staring me right in the face was none other than Merlin.

"Why, look who's here!" I said to myself, feeling both surprise and relief. "Merlin, you sly dog, long time no see!" I sniffed Merlin over good, breathing in that peculiar smell of his, a smell that has always reminded me of sour apples. And then Merlin cupped my face firmly between his hands and looked me straight in the eye.

"Yes, Cabal," he said, "it *has* been a long time since we've seen one another. But I'm pleased to see that my favorite canine is looking fit." Then Merlin gave me a big wink!

It took a few seconds for me to put two and two together, but when I had, I realized that Merlin's words were in reply to what I had been *thinking*! Now wait just a minute! I thought. Can Merlin "hear" my thoughts when they're still inside my head? Is this weird old geezer some kind of a *thought reader*?

"Don't go fretting yourself," Merlin said with a smile, "but it's true; sometimes I do understand what's going on in people's minds. And for some reason, Cabal, your thoughts come through more clearly than most. But don't go fretting yourself. It's just a little talent I was born with, and one I'd prefer that people didn't know about. So if you won't go telling my secrets," Merlin said, giving me another wink, "I won't go telling yours. Fair enough?" I just cocked my head sideways and stared at the strange old fellow.

"Cabal," Merlin went on after a moment, "I'd hoped to find Arthur here. I need to talk to him, and I don't want anyone knowing about it. That's why I came in through the window. But I also need to talk to *you*, Cabal, so listen carefully. First of all, you must let Arthur know that I've left this for him." Merlin held up a small piece of parchment that had some writing on it. He let me sniff it good, and then he lifted a corner of Arthur's sleeping pallet and tucked it underneath.

"See where I've put this? You *must* let Arthur know about it the moment he gets back. And now the second thing, Cabal, which is just as important—so listen carefully. Cabal, I need you to stay very close to Arthur the whole time we're in London. Stay beside him every moment you can. And keep a sharp lookout. Your master may be in *great peril!*— there are people in London who intend to harm him if they get the chance.

"That's why I've let you in on my little mind-reading secret, Cabal. Situations may arise when I'll need to know exactly what you're thinking. And I want you to know that in an emergency you can get a message to me that way. Let's hope that by working together we'll be able to protect Arthur from any real harm. Now *don't forget!* These are matters of the gravest importance. Do you understand?"

"Of *course* I understand!" I shouted back at Merlin inside my head, feeling a little insulted by the suggestion that

I might not. "Of *course* I understand! I'm not some sort of dumb bunny, you know!"

"No, no, Cabal, that's quite all right," Merlin replied softly, running his fingers through the fur on my chest. "Of course you're not a dumb bunny. You're a very bright boy. I've known that since that time you helped save Arthur's life at the Red Castle. But remember, Cabal, Arthur really needs your help, now more than ever. Whatever you do, don't let Arthur down."

In a flash Merlin had gone out through the window, and it was a couple of days before he turned up again. But what a couple of days they were!

An hour or so after my visit from Merlin, Arthur returned from dinner. He'd brought me a very choice bone and some bread scraps soaked with gravy. Yumm. But believe it or not, I ignored this gourmet meal (for the moment, anyway). As soon as Arthur was in the room, I took the edge of his cloak between my teeth and pulled him toward his sleeping pallet. Then I scrabbled at the floor beside the pallet and whined a polite little whine.

"What's got into you, Cabal?" Arthur said, puzzled by my odd behavior. Then, stooping over to see what all the fuss was about, he raised the corner of the pallet. When he spotted the parchment, his eyes got big. And they *really* got big when he'd deciphered Merlin's horrid scrawl.

Arthur ran his eyes over what Merlin had written a couple of times. Then he stepped over to the wall bracket and set the parchment alight! He held it in his hand while it burned, and only when the flame was starting to scorch his fingers did he drop the remaining bit on the floor and stamp on it. Then he picked up the tiny fragment, inspected it, rolled it between his fingers, and flipped it up into the air. I leaped up and snagged it, gave it a chew, and gulped it down. So much for Merlin's message!

Arthur sat beside me and stroked my side. He seemed pensive and a little worried, but he didn't tell me a blessed thing about Merlin's message. Couldn't he *tell* I was dying to know what was going on? Goodness, Arthur, you know your silly old fur-dog better than that, don't you?

"Cabal," Arthur said to me a few minutes later, "do you know what tomorrow is?" I just cocked my head sideways and looked at him. "Tomorrow is the winter solstice, the shortest day of the year, and tomorrow night will be the longest night of the year. People used to call it Mid-Winter's Day, though it seems to us that winter is just getting started. It used to be a special day—that's what Merlin says. Christmas is our special day now.

"And guess what, Cabal, it's only four more days till Christmas. Maybe I'll give you a special present. You have been a *pretty* good dog this year. Not *perfect*, mind you, but *pretty* good," Arthur said with a grin. The guy was pulling my leg, don't you think?

That night I lay beside Arthur watching him as he slept. I thought about many things as I lay there in the dark, doing the job that Merlin expected me to do. I thought about our home far off in the west and the other dogs in Tom kennelman's kennels. I wondered how they were doing. And I thought about the things we'd seen on the journey to London. And I thought about Merlin, that strange old fellow, and about his concern for Arthur's safety. Merlin, I could tell, loved Arthur almost as much as I do. Only when I knew that Emrys was up and starting his morning chores did I dare to doze off. And when I did, I dreamed a dream I often have—the dream of how Arthur and I first came to know each other.

V   My Dream of Arthur

It was long ago and I was back at the Red Castle, where the cold winter wind was whispering through the cracks and crannies of the kennel. My brothers and sisters and I were snuggled up warmly against the fur of our mother's belly when we were startled into wakefulness by the sudden appearance of bright lights. I looked up sleepily, blinking against the brightness of the lights, and there gazing down at us were several people. I knew by then what people were, but it made me nervous to be around them. As they stood there looking at us and talking, I could smell their different smells. I was used to the smell of Tom kennelman, but the smells of the others were new and strange.

"Well, Kei, which one would you like?" said a tall bearded man. He stood with one hand on the shoulder of the boy beside him. The boy reached down and scooped up one of my brothers.

"Look at this guy!" he said. "He looks like a wolf cub! Hello, Lupus!" My brother squirmed and twisted, but the boy just squeezed him all the harder. "My own little wolf," he laughed. "Doesn't he look just like a wolf, Merlin?"

"I should say so, Kei; yes, he bears a distinct resemblance to a young wolf."

86

This man looked older than the first man, and he had a shaggy gray beard. But the strangest thing about him was his peculiar smell, a smell that has always made me think of sour apples.

"So you want to call him Lupus, do you Kei?" said the older man.

"Don't you think that's perfect, Merlin?"

"It should do quite nicely," the man replied.

"What about you, then, Arthur?" the first man said, looking at the other boy. This boy was shorter than the boy named Kei, and all the time they'd been there he'd stood quietly beside the others.

"I'm not quite sure," the boy replied softly. There was silence in the kennel as the boy looked us over. Then he said, "Maybe that little reddish-brown one." Then he reached down and picked me up, and oh my goodness, was I ever scared! It was all I could do to keep from peeing. But the boy's hands were warm and gentle, and he didn't hurt me at all.

"Hello, little fella," he said to me, cradling me in his arms. "*You're* no wolf cub, are you." I didn't know what he meant by that, but I hoped it was a compliment.

Then the other boy began to laugh. "Leave it to Arthur to pick the runt of the litter."

"Beggin' your pardon, young master Kei," said Tom kennelman. "He's a wee little one this day, but I'm a-thinkin' he'll not be stayin' so for long. He's after havin' very large paws, my lord."

"He does indeed!" shouted Kei. "Look at those clod-stompers! They're immense. They're big as Lupus's paws! Well, Arthur, what'll you call this mighty beast of yours? Ursus? Or maybe Castor would be more like it. He looks like a young castor to me."

"Merlin," said the first man, "I see Kei's managed to learn a little something from his Latin lessons. By the way," he said more softly, "what does castor mean?"

"Beaver, my lord Ector, it means beaver."

"Ah," said the man named Ector.

"No . . . ," said the boy named Arthur, rubbing his chin. "I do rather like your suggestion of Ursus, but I can't have you naming *my* dog. Perhaps I'll should call him Equus," the boy said at last.

That brought another howl of laughter from the boy named Kei. "A runty little dog named horse!" he shouted gleefully. "Arthur, how absurd!"

"No . . . ," said Arthur still rubbing his chin, "no, . . . on second thought I don't think I'll call him Equus. He looks like such a humble little pup, I think I'd rather call him Cabal."

"*Now* you've hit on it, Arthur! Now you've got it right. For if that little runt of a dog is a horse, with those clod-stompers of his he's just the one for pulling a hay wagon."

To tell you the truth, I wasn't following all this business about names and animals and horses. That didn't matter to me. What mattered to me was that the boy called Arthur was holding me gently and stroking me softly. As far as I was concerned, he could call me anything he darn well pleased.

That night Lupus and I were taken away by our new masters. Lupus soon grew to love Kei, and I'd loved Arthur from that first moment when he'd held me so gently. Arthur has always been a kind and loving master to me. No dog has ever had a better one.

VI   A Short but Sweet Day

Maybe the next day was a bit short on daylight, but it certainly wasn't short on excitement, for Kei would be fighting in his very first tournament, a special tournament that was just for fledgling knights. Of course Kei had very high hopes for himself. You know Kei—always thinking he's hot stuff. But Kei really did have a lot of potential. He'd worked hard during his training at the Red Castle, and people who knew about these things considered him one of Britain's brightest young hopefuls. At an early age Kei had shown a natural talent for riding, and now he would be mounted on Brutus, a tried and true warhorse. I was pretty sure Kei would do fine in the jousting part of things. I wasn't so sure about the sword fighting part of it, though. It'd been a couple of years since Kei had bested Arthur in a sword fight—and Arthur wasn't even a knight yet!

And so early on the morning of Mid-Winter's Day, Kei and Emrys set off for the tournament field. A little later the rest of us—except for Lupus, whose turn it was to stay behind and guard our belongings—set off too. (I kind of suspected they didn't want Lupus around when Kei was out on the tournament field. He might get too excited and embarrass the heck out of us.)

I felt sorry for Hervey, whose broken arm was keeping him out of the competition. He was itching to be out there with the others, but there wouldn't be any tournaments for Hervey for a while yet. Arthur was itching to be out there too, but since he wouldn't be knighted until next fall, he'd have to wait even longer than Hervey. But at least Arthur had something to look forward to—for later on there would be minor tournaments just for the squires. No one was thinking much about that just then—except for Arthur and me and assorted squires all over the city of London.

Now Kei was out on the field, riding up and down on the prancing Brutus, warming up with all the other young knights. He looked very grand decked out in Sir Ector's colors. He wore a silver surcoat over his chain-mail shirt; it had red upside-down vees against a silver background. Yes, Kei looked splendid out there with his lance and sword, his shield and helmet. I felt myself puffing up with pride. Hey, everybody, I wanted to bark, that's my master's brother out there, that one over there, the handsome fellow in silver!

Many eyes were on Kei, but he was by no means the only impressive-looking young knight on the field. There were quite a few likely-looking lads out there, and one of them made me especially nervous, a broad-shouldered chap garbed all in green.

"That young fellow in green," said Sir Ector at just that moment, "is called Sir Sagramore. They say his uncle brought him all the way from Constantinople. He's the odds-on favorite today." Whew! *Constantinople!* Did that ever sound grand! I had no idea where Constantinople was. But I was guessing Sir Sagramore had travelled a lot farther than we had.

So people considered Sir Sagramore to be the odds-on favorite, did they? Well, we'd just have to see what Kei would say about that. I sat there beside Arthur with my paws crossed, hoping to bring Kei good luck. That was something Arthur often advised me to do—"Keep your paws crossed, Cabal," he'd say, "and maybe we'll be in luck." So I kept my paws crossed, hoping Kei would be in luck.

After a lot of silly preliminaries—which included more blowing of trumpets than my ears would have preferred!— the tournament finally got going. The first phase of it involved a series of one-on-one jousts. Two knights would pair off and ride to the opposite ends of the field. Then they'd come charging down a runway, each one trying to knock the other off his horse. It was exciting to see the colorful horses and riders come thundering down the field towards each other, and it was quite a sight to see a knight go flying through the air and come crashing down in a heap.

Kei got off to a great start, unhorsing five or six guys in a row. On each charge he seemed to know just the right time to raise his lance and the perfect spot to place it. His aim and timing were impeccable. Brutus could always be counted on to do his part, and the two of them made an excellent team. But now it had all come down to just two knights, Kei and Sagramore. All the others had bit the dust. I was getting really jumpy, for I wasn't sure how Kei would fare against this powerful young knight who'd come all the way from Constantinople.

Then Brutus thundered down the runway toward Sir Sagramore's charging warhorse. Arthur was squeezing my neck so tight I thought I might choke to death. I guess he didn't realize what he was doing; I guess he was just as excited as I was. And then, whoosh, before you could say Joseph of Arimathea, it was all over and done with. And there, lying flat on the ground, was a very green and dusty looking Sir Sagramore.

Kei had knocked the poor bloke head over heels. A wild cheer went up from many of the spectators, especially those sitting around us, and a groan rose up from some of the others. They must have been friends of Sir Sagramore—or maybe they'd been foolish enough to bet on the odds-on favorite.

But now came the scary part. For now that the jousting was over, Kei was suppose to dismount and challenge Sir

Sagramore to a sword fight. If Sir Sagramore refused, or if he was too injured to fight, then Kei would be the winner. But this time there was no such luck (so much for my crossed paws!), for an angry young Sir Sagramore leapt up on his feet and whipped out his sword, eager to continue the fight.

Soon we heard the sounds of cold steel clashing against cold steel. There was a lot of thrusting and parrying, hacking and whacking. Sir Sagramore was much bigger than Kei, and he went on the offensive right away. Kei was constantly backpedaling, doing his best to fend off Sir Sagramore's blows.

And then an amazing thing happened. From the beginning, a lot of folks had been cheering for Sir Sagramore; but as the fight went on, more and more of them started pulling for Kei. That was because Kei was putting up a remarkably good fight. It had been clear from the beginning that Sagramore was miles better than Kei in sword fighting. But Kei wasn't about to give in without a struggle. He was fighting for all he was worth.

"He's a plucky one, that one in silver," I heard someone exclaim.

And then someone else shouted, "Come on, lad, show 'em what we're made of in Herefordshire!"

"He mayn't have great skills," came another voice, "but he's a stout-hearted young feller, no doubt about it!"

"He's a game one, all right, indeed he is."

"*I* think he's very handsome," said a young female voice.

"How could you possibly know *that*," said a gruff male voice, "when the fellow's vizor is down?"

"I just know, that's all," the young female replied pertly.

Kei was proving himself a courageous fighter in what was clearly an uphill struggle. I was proud of him the whole time—proud when he blocked a dozen blows with his poor battered shield; proud when he surprised his foe and landed a strong clean hit on Sagramore's right shoulder, nearly causing him to drop his sword; proud when Sagramore gave him such a buffet on his helmet that his knees buckled under him and he slumped down to the ground. I was proud of Kei when he was forced to accept defeat and yield his weapon to the superior swordsman.

Kei had more people cheering for him in defeat than Sir Sagramore had cheering for him in victory.

"Bravely fought, lad, bravely fought!"

"I must say, that was a jolly fine match. The lad in silver really showed his mettle."

Sir Sagramore was awarded top honors for the day, with Kei coming in second. I wasn't quite sure why it should have been that way, since Kei had been better than all the others, including Sir Sagramore, in the jousting. But I guess the sword fighting must have counted for more. Anyway, Kei had acquitted himself very well, and although he'd taken quite a battering from the brash Sir Sagramore, he was in high spirits after it was all over and done with. And he'd won a lot of hearts with the brave show he'd put on.

One of the hearts he'd won was that of the young woman who'd called Kei handsome. I saw her come over to Kei, accompanied by a grumpy-looking older man, and say something to Kei that I couldn't quite hear. Whatever it was, it caused something to happen that I'd never seen before—it caused a huge blush to spread all over Kei's happy-looking face.

VII   The Truth About
Cats and Dogs

Supper that evening involved some serious celebrating, for in our eyes Kei was truly a hero. Even though he hadn't quite won top honors, he'd come away with the next best thing, the respect of everyone who'd seen him.

Truthfully, Kei had done better than I'd thought he would, and the thought was crossing my mind that maybe I should revise my opinion of the guy. But then another thought crossed my mind—if Kei had done so well, how well would *Arthur* have done? I know I'm biased when it comes to comparing Kei and Arthur, but I also know that Arthur is much better at these things—especially the sword-fighting—than Kei will ever be, even in his dreams!

That evening we sat in the dining room of the Mermaid Inn for quite a while celebrating Kei's success. His deeds had turned him into an instant celebrity, and a lot of people, some we didn't even know, came to meet the young hero and congratulate him.

Among our visitors were Sir Bedivere, Sir Lucan, and Sir Griflet. I hadn't seen them at the tournament, but word must get around fast in London because they were well up on the day's events. They came in together and gave Kei some kind words and congratulatory pats on the back. Praise from those three was high praise indeed, and I could tell that Kei was firmly seated on Cloud Nine.

But some of the folks who stopped by made me suspicious. I couldn't help wondering what they were up to. It seemed like they wanted to get chummy with us just because we were on our way to becoming important. But there was one visitor who took us completely by surprise. This was none other than King Nentres of Garlot, one of the lesser kings who was hoping to be the next High King. King Nentres entered the dining room of the Mermaid Inn with three silent but well-armed guards who never left his side. He was a slender man with a sleek black beard and glittery black eyes that darted about the room. He had a friendly smile pasted on his lips, and his speech was full of praise for the fresh young knight from the west who'd become the talk of the town.

Now, what is this fellow up to, I wondered? Is this just a pleasant little social call? I really had my doubts. King Nentres seemed to be taking stock of our entire party. He was sizing up Kei, sizing up Sir Ector and Sir Rhys, and most of all, he was sizing up Arthur! He didn't study Arthur for long, but he took a good little look, and I had the impression that what he saw made him nervous. Just after that, King Nentres said his farewells. Then he and his three silent henchmen trudged off into the night.

Our most pleasing visitor from Kei's point of view was the young woman who'd spoken to him after the tournament. This time she didn't speak to him at all—that was left up to the older man who turned out to be her father. On this occasion the man set his gruffness aside and spoke very graciously to Kei and Sir Ector. He introduced himself as the Duke of Clarence and his daughter as Rosalette. He struck me as an okay chap, even though he didn't let Rosalette get in a single word. But while she didn't actually speak to Kei, *her* eyes and *his* eyes were carrying on quite a conversation, if you know what I mean!

Also among the folks who turned up was Taliesin the Bard, the fellow we'd met long ago in the forest. And he'd already composed a song about Kei's deeds in the tournament!—now that's what I call being a fast worker! Taliesin wanted Kei to be the first one to hear it, and it wasn't a bad little ditty, either. The words weren't so great, but the tune was catchy, and for the next several days the darn thing kept running around in my head.

On the twenty-first day of December,
In the very last month of the year,
Young lads sallied forth to do battle,
Young men who had never known fear.
To the lists they came riding in splendor,
In armor that looked oh so grand;
And eager to start the encounter,
They waited with lance firm in hand . . . .

As Taliesin was singing, one very sleepy dog had begun to nod off. I didn't mean to be rude, but the shortest day of the year had been a very long one. But as a matter of fact, it wasn't quite over.

The action started a couple of hours after we'd gone to bed. I was lying by Arthur, not quite awake and not quite asleep, when Lupus roused himself from his blankets and went over to the back window. I was soon there beside him, peering out into the night. What had drawn Lupus's attention was *cats*—the very same cats I'd noticed the day we arrived. They were having quite a shindig out by the stables, and the sight of those cats frolicking out there soon had the two us all a-dither. When Lupus couldn't stand it any longer, he flew right out the window, not worrying about the ten-foot drop. And in the next second, I'd followed his example.

As I raced across the courtyard, I heard quite a commotion up ahead of me. Lupus had already set to work, and now feline fun-time was coming to an end. But in case you might feel a little sorry for those cats, let me remind you of something you already know—all cats need to be taken down a peg or two now and then. If they aren't, they get too darn big for their britches. And there's nothing worse than a stuck-up cat! Cats need to have their feathers ruffled once in a while. That's surely one of the reasons why God made dogs.

Lupus was breaking up that cat party in a jiffy, and now cats of all shapes and sizes were tearing out of there like bats out of hell. A few stalwarts were still standing their ground. But when they heard reinforcements charging up from the rear—namely me—they chose discretion over valor and took to their paws. And then the chase was on, with those wily town cats leading Lupus and me up and down the narrow lanes and alleyways of darkest London. Around and around we went until my chest was on fire. And then, as if by magic, they were gone—like a river mist in the morning sun. And all about us the night was eerily still.

Lupus and I stood there on trembling legs, our chests heaving, our steamy breath visible in the night air. And that was when we began to hear some completely different sounds, sounds that sent shivers up my back. *What in blazes were they?* We stood there with our heads cocked, listening to the weirdest sounds—high-pitched squeals coming one on top of another from a myriad of small voices. Bats? No, not bats; the sounds weren't high enough, and they were too jumbled on top of each other.

Lupus and I stood looking down a dark little lane that slanted toward the river. As nervous as these sounds were making us, our curiosity was too strong to resist. We were soon inching our way along the little lane, and the closer we got to the river, the louder the sounds.

When we reached the end of the lane, there in plain view were the creatures that were making these hideous sounds. But what the devil *were* they? They were nearly as large as squirrels or rabbits, but they certainly weren't squirrels or rabbits. They looked more like huge mice—mice with long pointy snouts and glowing red eyes. They had long whip-like tails and large ugly teeth, and they were teeming all over something. When we got closer, we could see it was a rubbish heap. They were ransacking it for all they were worth, and what an unholy mess they were making! And what an unholy racket! The squeals we'd been hearing were squeals of delight.

Lupus and I stood there for a moment, fascinated by the incredible frenzy of activity. Then my brother and I looked at each other in silent communication, and we both knew we were of one mind. Lupus had a huge grin on his face, a grin I can only describe as a poop-eating grin. And that grin was conveying one very clear message—it was saying, "Let's Do It!"

Before you could say Joseph of Arimathea, "do it" was what we did. We charged into the midst of those foul-smelling, foul-sounding critters, barking and snarling our heads off. And there was a flutterment and a scufflement and then those lousy stinking *rats*—for that's what those scuzzy little monsters were—headed for the hills. Some of them scurried up the ropes of ships. They were the smart ones, for Lupus and I couldn't go after them. But we rampaged about on the wharf for a while, snarling and snapping and snipping. You might say the fur was really flying!

When the remnants of the rat pack had skittered off into the dark, Lupus and I did our own poking about in that rubbish heap—which stank to high heaven! I found one particularly horrible substance that I had a powerful urge to roll in. I didn't know what it was, but it gave me an aroma I was certain would make folks sit up and take notice.

Later, after we'd wreaked enough havoc for one night, Lupus and I trotted along the little city lanes, trying to figure out where in the heck we were. And that was when a terrible thought came crashing down on me. Good gravy! I thought, look at me! Traipsing about London in the wee hours of the night, having the time of my life with my madcap brother, when I was *supposed* to be guarding Arthur! Good gravy, what a dumb bunny I am! I hope to heaven Arthur is okay!

Pretty soon I figured out where we were, thank goodness, and Lupus offered no complaint when I stepped up our pace. Before long our lodgings on Candlewick Street had come into view, and then, just as we were coming through the stables, we heard someone shouting in a high, frightened voice—"Vinegar! Vinegar! Help me, Vinegar!" Someone was dangling from an old wisteria vine that twisted along the walls and around the windows of the rooms on the higher floors of the inn. From the look and sound of him, I guessed he was a little tyke, maybe five or six years old. Whoever he was, he was definitely in a jam.

Lupus and I rushed over to the area beneath where the little fellow was hanging and added our loudest barks to his frantic cries of "Vinegar! Vinegar!" Heads began popping out of windows, and people began shouting at us, some of them shouting rude things that I didn't appreciate at all.

Then I saw a young man climb out of a window and start making his way along the side of the building, clambering about as sure-footedly on the wisteria vine as if it were the rigging of one of the ships on the Thames. He worked his way along the building, and in a few moments he'd reached the panic-stricken boy who kept right on shrieking "Vinegar!"

He had quite a time wrenching the boy's hands free of the vine, but when he'd managed it, he hoisted the boy onto his shoulder and descended safely to the courtyard.

And whatta ya know—the rescuing hero was Arthur! Way to go, master, I barked out, way to go! That's my master! I barked as loud as I could to the faces that peered out of the windows all around the courtyard. Arthur tried to comfort the little squirt but that was no easy task. "Where's Vinegar, where's Vinegar," he kept on sobbing. And then he shouted "I WANT VINEGAR!" at the top of his lungs. Goodness, what a racket the little twerp was making!

All of a sudden he cried out, "Vinegar! Oh, Vinegar!" He tore himself loose from Arthur and threw his arms around the thighs of the young woman who was striding across the courtyard. At that point the boy's sobs of fear became sobs of relief. Arthur just stood there awkwardly while she soothed the little boy. Then she turned to Arthur.

"I am truly grateful to you for rescuing my pesky little brother," she said. "He's *always* getting into scrapes like this—it's *terribly* exasperating! But he doesn't usually do it in the middle of the night!" Then turning to the little boy she said, "What were you doing, Mellie? What made you get out of bed and tumble out of the window?"

"I had a *bad dream*, Vinegar," the little boy sobbed. "I had a *terrible* bad dream. Dragons were after me, and they were *big* and *smelly*!"

At the word "smelly," Arthur and the young woman both looked directly at me, which I suppose might have been because of what Lupus and I had been doing a little earlier. But the young woman had her hands full right then dealing with the distraught little boy, and Arthur's attention, it was plain to see, had become riveted on no one but the young woman.

"My name's Arthur," he finally blurted out, since there was no one around to perform a proper introduction. "Are you, uh, called Vinegar?" he asked, with a slight hesitation in his voice.

"Oh no!" she laughed. "That's just what Melleas calls me—he's done that since he first learned to talk. My name is Gwinevere," she said. "My father is King Leodegrance of Carmelide. We've come to London for the choosing of the new High King."

"Why, what a coincidence!" Arthur replied, with a silly grin all over his face. "That's why *we've* come to London, too." Yes, I thought, that's why we've come to London—us and about ten thousand other folks! What a coincidence indeed!

VIII Lashed but not Leashed

The first thing Arthur did the next morning was give me a bath. Before we'd even eaten breakfast, Arthur had me out in the stables in an old tub filled with water. He gave me the best scrubbing I'd had in a month of Sundays. It reminded me of the freezing baths Old Tom used to give us back at the Red Castle when Lupus and I were pups. The water wasn't *quite* that cold, but it was plenty cold enough, thank you very much!

As Arthur was toweling me off, Merlin slipped silently into the stables. By the way he was acting, I could tell he didn't want to be seen. He stayed in the shadows and beckoned for Arthur to follow him to an empty stall. Then he whispered so softly to Arthur I only caught a few of his words—"danger," "dagger," "brooch," and "King Lot."

When Merlin had finished with Arthur, it was my turn to have a talking to. Merlin looked at me sternly and motioned for me to follow him. I did, but I wasn't happy about it, because I had a good idea what I was in for. When we were alone, Merlin took my chin firmly in his hand and looked me square in the eye. I could tell he knew what Lupus and I had been doing the night before. And I could tell that he was plenty irked.

"Now, listen to me, Cabal!" Merlin said sharply. "It seems that I've misjudged you. I gave you a very important job, but you went and botched it! I thought I could count on you. I thought *Arthur* could count on you. If you can't be trusted to stand by Arthur when he needs you, perhaps we'll have to find someone else who can. Is that what you want?"

Goodness, Merlin, that question hardly needs an answer! Of *course* I don't want you to find someone else for Arthur! Those were my thoughts, but I knew this was no time to be giving Merlin any back chat. And the truth was, I already felt plenty guilty about what'd happened last night. Merlin's tongue-lashing, plus the guilt I already felt, caused my poor old tail to droop right down between my legs. It was all I could do to glance up at Merlin sheepishly.

But to my great relief, Merlin's scowl suddenly disappeared; and then Merlin the Wizard gave me a great big smile. Whew, I thought, sunshine after a storm!

"Fortunately," Merlin said, "no real harm's been done *this* time." Then he gave me a gentle rub behind my ears with his sour-apple smelling hands. "And I know nobody's perfect, Cabal. No," he sighed, "I certainly know *that*."

"Merlin," I said in my mind, hoping he could still read my thoughts, "what I did last night was terrible. It was thoughtless and selfish. And I swear on the grave of my father that never again will I fail my master and liege lord in his hour of need."

Merlin laughed out loud. "I'm not laughing at you, Cabal, but it sounds as if you've been listening to too many silly tales of chivalry. Nonetheless, I accept your noble vow. And Cabal," he said looking me right in the eye, "I intend to hold you to it."

Arthur poked his head into our stall and gave us a quizzical look. Who could blame him? It must have seemed pretty strange to see a wizard and a dog deep in a one-sided conversation.

"Arthur," said Merlin, sounding a little embarrassed, "Cabal and I have just finished our chat."

"Uh... okay...," said Arthur, still looking perplexed. "That's good, because I'm starvingly hungry; and breakfast is now being served in the dining room. You coming, Cabal?"

Despite the fact that I should have been feeling cold, damp, and miserable—from the much-hated bath Arthur had given me and the much-deserved tongue-lashing Merlin had given me—I leaped up on my master and licked his face. Arthur, who I loved more than my life, was alive and well! He was going to stay that way if it was the last thing I ever did! And besides, it was time for breakfast.

The next few hours were pretty uneventful. Once Arthur and I had eaten, we just hung around the inn, not doing much of anything. I was a little surprised by this, for Arthur was a fellow who liked to be doing things or going places. And then, smart dog that I am, I figured out what was going on. All the time that we were just hanging around, Arthur was on the lookout for something. Actually, it wasn't some *thing* he was on the lookout for, it was some *one*! Arthur was watching for the young woman he'd met the night before.

A little before noon he got his wish. That was when Gwinevere and Melleas finally came down for breakfast. I don't know how anyone could go so long without eating, but I guess they must've slept in on account of the late-night doings I've told you about. When they came down to the dining room, Arthur just *happened* to run into them. Arthur, I thought, *you* are the original sly dog!

After they exchanged polite "good mornings," Gwinevere asked if we'd eaten, or if we would like to join them. Well, what a surprise! Neither Arthur nor I had any objection to having a second breakfast.

Within minutes Arthur and Gwinevere were chatting and joking as if they'd been chums for years. I was amazed to see Arthur become so talkative so suddenly. He was usually quite shy in the presence of women. Maybe there was something special about this particular young woman that changed all that, for right before my eyes my master had become quite the lady charmer! Way to go, master, I thought with a grin, way to go.

Gwinevere was supposed to be watching Melleas that day, and Arthur volunteered to keep her company while she did. Gwinevere said she would like that very much. Then she took her eyes off of Arthur—for once—and gave *me* a smile. She was checking me out good, and this time I seemed to meet with her nose's approval. And *now* I knew why Arthur had given me that dratted bath!

The December day was clear and crisp, a perfect day to be out and about in the City of London. Gwinevere and

Mellie and Arthur wrapped themselves in woolen cloaks, and then the four of us set out to see the sights. As we walked along, I recognized some of the lanes that Lupus and I had wandered the previous night. Soon we were strolling beside the River Thames, moving away from the Tower of London and toward a strange-looking bridge which, reasonably enough, was called London Bridge. All across it were stalls and shops where folks were selling everything under the sun. But what intrigued me most of all were the fish!

London must have been the fish capital of the world. Back at the Red Castle we'd eaten fish now and then, but the puny little things Emrys and Davi caught in the River Wye couldn't hold a candle to the amazing fish they had in London—fish of every shape and size imaginable. The largest ones were strung on ropes, hanging in the sun in all their smelly glory. Other kinds were piled on carts where women were pawing through them, trying to find the best ones. Still others lay in great heaps of straw on the ground. My goodness, how their fishy aromas filled the London air!

We threaded our way through the throng of bargain-hunters and reached the other side. On this side of the river the buildings weren't so packed together, and we could get a good look at the City of London. We stared across the water at the great buildings of London. All across the city elegant spires reached toward the heavens. But nothing could match the towers and pinnacles of St. Paul's Cathedral, soaring magnificently above the city.

But all the while we'd been strolling along on this pleasant little outing, I *wasn't* just being your run-of-the-mill London tourist. Oh no, I most assuredly *wasn't*. Cabal, the gentle grass-eating dog, was being a very vigilant guard dog. All the time since we'd left the Mermaid Inn I'd been keeping a sharp eye out, watching for any suspicious-looking characters or anything else that seemed out of the ordinary. And it wasn't long before I'd begun to notice something that *was* out of the ordinary.

There was a particular man, a rather tall and gaunt-looking fellow who was all muffled up in a gray hooded cloak, who kept turning up wherever we went. He had a long wooden staff that he sometimes leaned against, so he appeared to be elderly. But in my opinion he was a very shifty-looking character. Wherever we went, he was usually close by. And when I would turn in his direction to get a good look at him or to sniff him over good, he'd move quickly away and pretend to be heading someplace else. Then a little later, there he'd be again. This, I thought, is not good.

As we were re-crossing London Bridge, Melleas announced that he was hungry. Gwinevere checked out the various stands and came back with a bag of hard green apples for us to snack on.

"Not *apples*!" shouted Mellie. "Oh Vinegar, you *know* I don't like *apples*!" (To be honest, I thought Gwinevere could have done a little bit better myself.) Looking peeved, Gwinevere went over to another stall and tried again, and this time she did a lot better. This time she came back with a sack full of fresh-roasted chestnuts—yumm! Now Mellie and I were a lot more cheerful.

After we'd dealt with the chestnuts, we retraced our steps on the city side of river. In the open space that ran beside the Thames things had livened up in the last hour. Now there were food sellers beside their carts urging folks to come and buy their wonderful whatever-they-weres. Bonfires were crackling and sparks were shooting way up into the sky, and crowds of people huddled about them, laughing and chatting.

A lot of the folks meandering along the river were just like us—folks who'd come to the city from faraway places to be present at a very special event. And like us, they were enjoying the city on a lovely winter's day. The people in London, whether Londoners or not, were feeling excited. The fact that it was almost Christmas was one reason to be excited, but these folks had an even better reason. Because if there was any truth to the Bishop of London's dream, the people of Britain were about to have a new High King. Now *that* was something a fella could get excited about!

Arthur had his own reasons for being excited, for he had found himself a wonderful new friend. She was a friend, I was beginning to suspect, like no friend Arthur had ever had before. But as for me, right at that moment I was excited for a completely different reason—because that man I've told you about, the old fellow with the staff who was all wrapped up in a cloak, the bloke who'd been dogging our footsteps all day long—was back on the scene again. He hadn't been around for a while, and I was hoping we'd seen the last of him. But now he was back, and now he was drawing near.

But I was on to the rascal! And if it was trouble he wanted, it was trouble he was going to get—trouble by the name of Cabal, the gentle grass-eating, butt-kicking dog! And just as I was thinking that thought, that's when the trouble started.

As my eyes were glued to the fellow in the gray cloak, all of a sudden my nose began flashing me a very different message, a message of the greatest urgency. All of a sudden I smelled a startling smell, a smell that was burned deep into the smell cells of my brain, a smell that brought rushing over me the most powerful feelings of anger. It also brought rushing over me memories of our little room in the Red Castle and a night long ago when Arthur and I had been the targets of a vicious intruder's malice.

In a flash my nose jerked my head away from the man in the cloak and in a totally different direction. My attention was directed to an ugly little man with little rat eyes, a pointy rat nose, and a little rat chin—to a stinking piece of vermin who was preparing to pounce on Arthur.

And that's what he did. Or rather, that's what he *tried* to do. Because as quick as he pounced, it wasn't quick enough to avoid a brave and noble beast who was a pretty good pouncer in his own right. Yes, there was a brave and noble beast there that day who leaped into the air and grabbed that villainous piece of vermin before he could initiate his evil intentions.

The smell of this horrible being had driven me into a furious rage. Believe me, red was the color I was seeing just then. And perhaps the experience I'd had the night before with all those stinking rats had made me something of an expert at putting verminous slime to flight.

My vicious leap succeeded in bringing my enemy down, but it didn't succeed in putting him out of commission. And so I ripped with my teeth at his forearm, causing him to drop the gruesome weapon he'd been gripping. "You butter-fingers!" I barked at him jeeringly. "You can't even hold on to a stupid little knife! That's twice you've had fumble-itis!"

As he tried to crawl away I rushed at him, and this time I took great pleasure in sinking my teeth deep into the calf of his leg. That made him squeal like an eel and squirm like a worm! Or rather, it made him squeal like the stinking rat he was! But what would you expect from a stinking piece of vermin! Then he made his ignominious escape, headfirst into the River Thames—ker-splosh!

All the while I was engaged in my little skirmish with this rat-faced fellow, there was a lot of action going on around me. My own stinking rat—as is the way with rats—had had some stinking companions of his own who'd come charging at Arthur. But I'm happy to say they met with stern resistance.

At the very moment that I was bringing down my detested enemy, Arthur quickly unsheathed his dagger. And not a moment too soon, for in the next second he was using his dagger to fend off a knife blow directed right at his chest. Arthur followed his neat parry with a powerful blow of his own, his dagger ripping through the cloak of his attacker, opening the flesh on the man's upper arm. "Excellent riposte, Arthur," I barked excitedly, while trying to stay focused on my own foul foe.

I wasn't able to see much of what happened to the third attacker, having my paws (and jaws) rather full at the time. But my ears stayed keenly attuned to all that was going on. And later I got a complete blow-by-blow account from Merlin. What happened, I learned, was that the third attacker was done in by a nifty piece of teamwork.

First of all, he was tripped up neatly by the old duffer in gray that I'd been so nervous about. For just as the man was making his move, that old geezer swung his staff against the attacker's ankles—bringing him down! And then as he was scrambling to get up again, Gwinevere entered the fray with her bag of apples. She swung it around in a big looping circle and then brought it up into the man's face—ker-smash! And then Melleas, who'd snatched up the old man's staff, finished the job by bashing the rotter right on his skull. I never imagined the little tyke could deliver such a whacking good buffet. Frankly, it makes me cringe just to think about it!

Anyway, that was *it* for our three attackers. My stinking enemy was now somewhere in the River Thames— where he could jolly well drown! The second attacker, the one who'd been so neatly fended off by Arthur, had dashed off down the walkway, running as crazily as a hare in the springtime. And the third blighter was down and out, perhaps for good, thanks to the bashing and battering he'd taken from Gwinevere and Melleas.

As to that old fellow in the gray cloak who'd been dogging our steps all day, well, I have to admit that in regard to him I'd been barking up the wrong tree. And I'm ashamed to admit how slow I was to figure him out. But by the time everything was over, I'd gotten a whiff of the man's sour-apple smell, a smell that could only belong to Merlin. But just as I was barking out a big "hello, Merlin!" the old geezer flashed me a wink and then disappeared amongst the crowd of silly gapers that'd gathered around us.

As we stood there catching our breaths and dusting ourselves off, who should come pushing through the crowd but Sir Bedivere, Sir Lucan, and Sir Griflet. Thanks a lot, boys, I thought, but *this* time around you're a day late and a farthing short. We've already polished off those slimy varlets—*all by ourselves*!

The three famous knights weren't much use to us at that point, but they were relieved to see that we were unharmed. And for good measure, they accompanied us back to the inn. They seemed quite impressed by the way we'd managed to fend off our attackers, which made me feel pretty good. But one thing I noticed was that Arthur didn't seem as much in awe of this trio of famous knights as he'd been before. I don't think it was out of any disrespect for them; I think it was because Arthur was experiencing a greater awareness of his own capabilities.

Back at the inn that night, after everyone had eaten their evening meal, Arthur made a big game out of bestowing well-deserved honors upon his three brave companions. He made Melleas kneel down on one knee and repeat after him an oath of chivalry. When Mellie had finally managed to get the oath *almost* right, Arthur tapped him on each shoulder and then on the top of his head with a large wooden serving spoon.

"In the name of St. Michael, St. Peter, and St. George," he said, "I hereby dub thee Sir Melleas de Lyttle. And for your deeds of derring-do, you shall henceforth be keeper of the royal staff, to be wielded in times of peril and in defense of your land and liege lord. Arise, Sir Knight! May you long uphold the tenets of chivalry to which you are now fully sworn."

Melleas was delighted at having been made a knight. And then he insisted on bestowing the very same honors upon me! That seemed kind of silly to me, but since it was important to Mellie, I tried to be patient about it—just as long as he tapped me *lightly* on the head and didn't go bashing me, the way he'd served that poor bloke earlier.

Mellie was actually quite gentle about it, although he managed to make a royal mess of the words. And then, after some quickly-whispered advice from Arthur, Mellie officially dubbed me "Sir Cabal le Savage." My first thought was that the title seemed a little inappropriate for a gentle grass-eating dog like me. But my second thought was—maybe not!

Arthur wanted to knight Gwinevere also, but she absolutely refused.

"I will be no man's vassal," she declared. "If my liege lord insists upon granting me a position of honor, then he must make me a princess at the least. And I would like it even better," she said, "if he chose to make me a queen."

part III

"... since I am a dog,
beware my fangs."
– *William Shakespeare*

I Something's Fishy

Arthur and I had a lovely sleep-in the next morning, aided by a change in the weather. When the gurgling of my digestive juices finally roused me from slumber, I yawned, took a big doggie stretch, and then sauntered over to the window to peek out at the world. To my astonishment, there was no world to peek out at! In fact, there was _nothing_ to peek out at—nothing except a blanket of gray. I was flummoxed until I realized it was _fog_—the thickest doggone fog I'd ever seen.

In a bit old sleepy-head Arthur joined me by the window. He rubbed the back of my head and stared out at that wall of fog.

"Goodness, Cabal, I wonder if there's anything out there? Maybe this little room of ours is all there really is."

Arthur must have been joshing, right? And yet it really did seem like we were completely alone in the world. But then the fog began to shift and thin in places, and then I could make out the shapes of buildings on the other side of Candlewick Street. Hooray, I barked, we're not alone! Arthur, there's a world out there after all, just waiting for us to conquer it!

Today, Arthur informed me as he was getting dressed, was Christmas Eve. A big banquet was planned for the middle of the day, and then everyone would attend an important church service at St. Paul's. If we wanted any breakfast, we would have to scrounge it for ourselves because none would be served. Also, he said, we couldn't have any meat because today was a fast day. I found that a little puzzling, considering the aromas that were wafting our way from the kitchens, aromas that bore a distinct resemblance to meat. "No meat?" I asked in my mind, looking at Arthur with my head cocked sideways.

"No meat," Arthur said, seeming to know my thoughts, "only fish, and fish isn't meat. But Cabal," he said, running his tongue around his lips, "wait till you taste that fish!"

Besides being Christmas Eve, today was also the Feast of Adam and Eve, which Arthur said was "a joyous fast." That meant that while we couldn't have meat, we could eat all the fish our little hearts might desire and our little tummies might hold. And that's what we did—we ate fish that was baked, fish that was broiled, fish that was fried, fish that was steamed, and fish that was stewed; we ate fish steaks and fish cakes and fish-flavored soup. Needless to say, it was a whale of a fish feast.

A lot of impressive guests joined us at the banquet. The Duke of Clarence and his daughter Rosalette had accepted Sir Ector's invitation, and their presence (especially Rosalette's) didn't make Kei unhappy. And King Leodegrance of Carmelide was there too, with Gwinevere and Melleas.

Their presence (especially Gwinevere's) didn't make Arthur unhappy. Also there was our friend Taliesin, along with his trusty harp.

As folks were gorging themselves on fish and bread and vegetables, us under-the-table denizens weren't faring too badly either. Lupus and I were benefiting from the assistance of our particular friends up topside, in addition to whatever we could nab for ourselves. Emrys and Davi and the other servants sat at a table beside ours, where they were making out pretty good too. Sir Ector never made a big deal out of social rank, and on this occasion everyone was being treated like one big happy family. No one even seemed to mind the eager beasts of the canine variety with whom they had to share their foot space.

There's just one other thing about the Christmas Eve banquet that I ought to mention. At one point fairly late in the meal a serving lad came in whom I hadn't seen before. He held a tray filled with steaming bowls of fish chowder that smelled mighty good! He stopped beside Arthur, picked out one of the little bowls, and placed it by Arthur's elbow. Then he asked who else would like some? Now why, I wondered, would he serve a bowl to Arthur and *then* ask if anyone wanted some? In the midst of all the merriment, no one seemed to have noticed this.

The lad handed out a few more bowls and then returned to the kitchen. Arthur glanced at the chowder with interest but decided he was too full to eat anything more. Emrys, never one to let good food go to waste, said he'd be glad to take the chowder off Arthur's hands, and Arthur passed it over. I didn't pay much attention to this little incident at the time, but I guess I should have, considering what happened later.

After everyone was finished eating, they pushed back their benches and sat there contentedly. That's when Taliesin took up his harp and started to play. He sang us a song that suited the occasion.

"Lu-lee, lu-lay, my dear little son,
Lu-lee, lu-lay, my heart's dearest one."
I saw a fair maiden, a hymn she did sing;
She rocked her small child, a lovely lording.
"Lu-lee, lu-lay, my dear little son,
Lu-lee, lu-lay, my heart's dearest one."

Rare hymns were heard at the holy child's birth,
The angels of heaven sang songs of great mirth.
"Lu-lee, lu-lay, my dear little son,
Lu-lee, lu-lay, my heart's dearest one."

Let us pray to the child and the Virgin so dear,
God's blessings on all who make Him good cheer.
Of each one He is Lord, He created all things;
Of all lords He is Lord, and King of all kings.
Sing "Lu-lee, lu-lay, lu-lee, lu-lay,"
For the child that was born on Christmas Day.

After the banquet everyone went to get ready for church, and that's when bells and chimes began ringing out all over London. The tintintabulations of those bells, bells, bells were enough to drive a poor dog crazy! "Cut it out!" I barked, "or you'll be shattering my poor reverberating skull!" But those damnable bells kept right on bonging away.

Emrys and Davi and Lupus and I went along with the others to the cathedral, though we wouldn't be attending the service. Navigating the streets of London in the fog was a very strange experience. At times we could barely see our paws in front of our faces; then the fog would thin out and blurry shapes would loom up in front of us. The eeriest thing was the way sounds were magnified. Just the simple clop, clop, clop of a horse's hooves sounded strange and ominous, echoing through that damp gray world.

Despite the fog we reached the cathedral without difficulty, and so did many others, for the open space in front was packed with the blurry forms of ordinary folks who'd come to catch a glimpse of Britain's finest nobles. Arthur and Kei and the others hurried on in, and then Emrys found us a good spot for watching the famous folks arrive. The fog had thinned out a good bit by then, so we had a clear view of all the goings-on.

Emrys and Davi were handy fellows to have around, for their whispered comments let me know who the folks were who were turning up for the service. But as a matter of fact, I was able to identify quite a few of them all by myself. I'm nobody's fool, I thought, standing tall and proud. I'm Cabal le Savage, one of Britain's wisest beasts.

As various groups appeared, the oohs and aahs of the crowd gave a good indication of their importance. One of the first groups included three of old King Uther's advisors—Sir Brastias, Sir Ulfin, and Sir Jordan. They were accompanying several women, one of whom I recognized. She was none other than Queen Igraine, King Uther Pendragon's widow.

I'd only seen Queen Igraine once before; that was that time when she and King Uther had visited the Red Castle. I'll never forget how she and the king came and sat with Arthur and me in our little chamber. I'll never forget how kind she was or how beautiful she looked. And I'll never forget how familiar she looked to me, even though I'd never seen her before.

After the Queen's party entered the cathedral there was a little lull before the next group arrived. And that was when Emrys started groaning and clutching his stomach.

"What's ailin' ya, Em?" croaked Davi. "You okay, mate?" It was obvious that Emrys *wasn't* okay. I was guessing he'd overdone it at the fish feast and now was paying for it. But the oohs and aahs of the crowd made us forget Emrys just then, for the next bunch of celebrities was arriving.

As these folks approached, a hush fell over the crowd. Goodness, I thought, there must be something special about *this* group. As I studied them, I saw that in their midst was a large man who looked familiar. I wracked my brain and then came up with the answer—it was King Uriens of Gore, one of the lesser kings. I'd seen him one time at the Red Castle, when he and King Lot had made a brief stopover there.

But nobody was paying much attention to King Uriens. Instead, all eyes were on the small woman who walked by herself out in front of him. "It's Morgan!" people were whispering, "It's Morgan le Fay!" As a matter of fact, I'd already guessed as much.

How could someone so small and slender, I wondered, appear so magnificent? For Morgan le Fay was certainly not a large person. Yet her movements commanded our attention, and she enthralled the gathering almost as if we had no choice in the matter. Morgan moved rapidly, taking long bold strides for such a short person, and her burgundy cape billowed out behind her. Her hood was tossed back, displaying her small lovely face. Her eyes were dark and brightly shining, and her very red lips carried just the hint of a smile. But to me the most striking thing about Morgan le Fay was her long dark hair which sparkled brilliantly against her burgundy cape. As I gazed at Morgan le Fay, two conclusions leaped into my mind—this woman was very pleased with herself; and this woman was nobody's fool.

Walking behind Morgan and beside King Uriens was a nice-looking lad of about Melleas' age. "That there's young Ewan," I heard Davi mutter. "There's those that say he's Uriens' son, and there's those that say he hain't," Davi went on, giving Emrys a big wink. But Emrys, I'm sorry to say, was more concerned just then with his belly than with the sights passing before our eyes.

King Mark of Lyoness and his party turned up next. For the first time, in among the oohs were some audible jeers.

King Mark, it appeared, didn't enjoy the same respect as the others. There were no women in this group, for King Mark's wife had died and he hadn't remarried. But the most impressive figure to me was a youth who was maybe a year or two younger than Arthur. He had hair the color of a ripe field of barley. Davi didn't know who he was, but I heard someone murmur, "The handsome lad's young Tristrem, King Mark's nephew."

In the next group was King Nentres of Garlot and his wife Mergit. She was Morgan le Fay's older sister, and although I could see a family resemblance, this woman possessed none of Morgan's magnetism. Mergit was attractive, but she lacked the commanding presence of her younger sister. No, in this group all eyes were on King Nentres, whom I've already told you about. He looked as sleek as a shiny black cat, and about as devious. This man, I knew, really wanted to be the High King of Britain, and I suspected he had plenty of tricks up his well-furred sleeves.

The last important group was that of King Lot of Lothian, a fellow against whom I'd developed a very big grudge. I've always tried to follow Arthur's advice about not bearing grudges. But when it comes to King Lot—sorry Arthur, there's no other way to put it—I hated the blighter's guts! I hated him because I believed in my heart that he was the one behind all the dirty deeds of that stinking rat-faced man! I believed in my heart that it was King Lot who'd been doing everything he could to harm my master Arthur.

What interested me most about this last group, though, wasn't King Lot—it was everyone else in his huge clan. King Lot was married to Margaux, the middle daughter of the Duke of Cornwall and the Lady Igraine. And there was no doubt that this auburn-haired woman was the true beauty from amongst that famous threesome. She was the beautiful one all right, and she darn well knew it. And yet she was making an effort not to make too much of her beauty. She was attired very simply in a plain black gown and cloak which allowed her own beauty to shine all the more brightly. This woman, I thought to myself, knows exactly what she's doing.

Along with King Lot and his wife was a bevy of little boys. Three of them were striding confidently in single-file behind their parents. The smallest one, who was just a toddler, was carried by a nursemaid.

"Now let's see here," mused Davi. "The strapping one's Gawain, methinks. And the tiny wee babe's little Gareth. But for the life o' me, I canna think o' the other lads," he said, scratching his chin. As King Lot's party filed past us, the oldest boy, the one Davi called Gawain, turned his head and looked in our direction. When his bright blue eyes spotted Lupus and me sitting there gazing at him, a big smile spread all across his face. He raised his hand and waved us a cheery greeting. There goes a boy, I said to myself, who is a true lover of dogs.

When the rest of the famous folks had gone in, the crowd outside the cathedral began to drift away. But we had other things to think about just then, for poor Emrys was doubled over in pain. "Best get ya back to the inn, old lad," said Davi. Emrys only moaned.

Just then my nose caught a whiff of a familiar sour-apple smell and my eyes caught sight of a man muffled up in a gray cloak. "Merlin!" I barked loudly. "Merlin, over here!" Merlin cast a bent-eyed glance in our direction, which I took to mean he didn't wish to be bothered. But I insisted. "Merlin, you old devil," I barked, "get your skinny carcass over here!"

Merlin came over to us, and I leaped up on him to show my appreciation. But Merlin wasn't in a cheerful mood. "*Not now*, Cabal!" he snarled. "This is no time for games!"

I didn't know why Merlin was being so snappish, but I didn't feel like backing down. "Listen, Merlin," I shouted inside my head, "you'd better get those thought-reading powers of yours working, because there's something you need to know. Emrys is *sick*! And if you ask me, Emrys has been *poisoned*!"

At that point Merlin sat up and took notice. He went quickly to Emrys and lifted his face. Then he felt his forehead and rolled back his eyelids. Merlin led Emrys over to the side of the street and made him bend over. He stuck something down his throat and then came the sounds of retching. Whew! Emrys' fish feast had been spewed out all over the street!

When Emrys was as empty as he was going to get, Merlin took something from his pouch and handed it to Davi. "Get him to bed, Davi. Steep these leaves in boiling water for fifteen minutes and make Emrys drink three cups of the tea every two hours." Emrys and Davi, their arms drapped about each other's shoulders, staggered off toward the Mermaid Inn, and Merlin, without a word of goodbye, rushed off to do whatever he'd been about to do when I first barked at him.

Then Lupus and I took up our vigil outside the cathedral, waiting for our masters Arthur and Kei.

II When the Fog Lifted

All that day the fog had been there, sometimes thicker, sometimes thinner. Now it was as thin as it had been at any time. Unfortunately, the air had turned colder, and it wasn't so pleasant for a pair of loyal dogs who were trying to sit there patiently. Lupus has never been very good at sitting patiently anyway, so to remedy our boredom and to put a little feeling back into our paddy-paws, Lupus and I set off on some harmless reconnoitering.

We sniffed our way around that huge cathedral, checking out its nooks and crannies. Now that the fog was nearly gone, I had a clear view of all the stone carvings; I could even make out some of the intricate designs in the stonework. We'd seen some impressive sights since we'd left the Red Castle—the minster at Gloucester, for one—but nothing that compared to St. Paul's Cathedral. My intrepid brother, though, only had eyes for the fine-feathered fowls that were fluttering everywhere—*pigeons*, the stupidest creatures that fly in God's firmament! The only thing I can say in their favor is that when they've been properly prepared, they make darn fine *eating*!

The pigeons of St. Paul's provided plenty of entertainment for my easily-amused brother. Spotting a cluster of them he'd make a mad dash, causing them to scatter in every direction. By the time he'd finished, the ground was filthy with pigeon poop!

Lupus and I meandered about St. Paul's for maybe fifteen or twenty minutes, and then we found ourselves right back in the large open space before the cathedral's west front. The fog was entirely gone now, and the air was cold and crystal clear. The last rays of the weak winter sun were slanting down into the cathedral square, and to our astonishment, they were shining upon something that hadn't been there before.

In the center of the open space was a huge black stone. On top of it, and somehow fastened into it, was a blacksmith's anvil like the ones I'd seen at the Red Castle. And slanting up out of it was a beautiful gleaming sword. Its golden hilt and shiny silver blade glowed in the waning daylight. "Peter, James, and John," I said to myself, "will wonders never cease!"

Folks had begun to gather about these strange objects, gabbing and gawking. Then they began pointing at something that *really* had them excited. Of course Lupus and I rushed over to see, and there, carved right into the side of the black stone, were *words*! I put my forepaws up on a smaller stone that was snuggled up against the huge one to get a better look. A fat lot of good it did me, of course, since I don't know how to read. But it didn't matter because there were a couple of geniuses there who *could* read, and they were soon telling everyone what was written on the stone. Here's what it said:

HE WHO PULLETH THE SWORD FROM THE STONE

IS THE TRUE-BORN KING OF BRITAIN.

As Lupus and I and our fellow onlookers were contemplating this marvel, the massive doors of the cathedral were thrown open—out poured the sounds of a joyous hymn of Christmas. Then through those wide-flung portals came a procession of robed figures. Heading the procession were youthful choristers singing like songbirds on a bright May morning. Behind them came a group of older lads who were belting out the hymn in their deeper voices. Then came a group of older men who were carrying holy objects.

Behind the procession of white and black and red-robed figures came all the folks we'd been watching earlier, Britain's finest nobles. And after them came Britain's lesser nobility, including Sir Ector, Sir Rhys, Sir Kei and Sir Hervey. And nearly last, but certainly not least, came my master Arthur.

Then all of the orderliness of that procession went flying out the window! For smack in the middle of the square where people couldn't avoid seeing it sat that wondrous sight. And as soon as folks saw it, thoughts of anything else went out of their heads. In almost no time at all, those fine and proper folks had become an excited mob crowding all about the huge black stone.

When the people closest to the stone got a glimpse of the writing, a murmur started up that spread across that crowd like a wave crossing water. Those folks were buzzing like a beehive that'd been whacked with a stick. Fortunately, there was a fellow there who rose to the occasion, and I do mean *rose*, for this fellow who was decked out in a fancy red robe leaped right up on top of the huge stone. He stood there with his arms held high, waiting for people to give him their attention. This athletic young clergyman, I soon discovered, was Bishop Baldwin, the Bishop of London, the very guy who'd had the vision I've told you about.

He was an impressive sight, standing there above the crowd with his arms held high. The people in front quieted down, and soon folks were shushing other folks all across the square. When there was complete silence, the bishop began speaking in a voice that resonated through the square.

"We have lifted our voices to the Almighty, and He has heard us. He knows our anguish and our plight. Because He is merciful, He is sending us help. Tomorrow is Christmas, a time of hope and renewal. Tomorrow we shall begin our search for Britain's new High King. Now, let us humble ourselves before the Lord. Now, let us offer Him silent prayers of thanksgiving."

Following the bishop's example, everyone in that huge crowd fell down on their knees, with their heads bowed. The cathedral square was so quiet you could have heard the tiniest mew of a new-born kitten. It was a wondrous sight. It was *so* wondrous that Cabal, the gentle grass-eating dog, wasn't able to bow his head. I *should* have, I know, but I couldn't take my eyes off the sight before me. But even though I couldn't bow my head, I think the Lord still knew I was as grateful as anyone there.

Following our silent prayers, the bishop addressed us again. "Tomorrow, after Christ's mass, we shall begin the trial of the stone. Until then, the stone will be guarded. No one must touch any of these precious objects until the trial begins. Let us pray that Britain will soon have her new High King."

As we stood there in the cathedral square in the gathering darkness, the good bishop told us to return to our lodgings and to be mindful of the wondrous events that had happened long ago on this holy night. He told us to be thankful for the Lord's tender mercies, tender mercies that extended to all His creatures. They *do*, I thought, they really *do*—even to creatures like me.

By the time we got back to the Mermaid Inn, I could smell the Christmas goose a-roasting. Yumm. Today's fish feast hadn't been too shabby, but I was really looking forward to tomorrow's meal. Roast goose, as you probably know, is as good as it gets. "Christmas is coming," I hummed inside my head, "the goose is almost done. Oh please, good sirs, if you'd be so kind, please give your doggies some."

When we got up to our rooms, there was Davi, waiting to tell Sir Ector about Emrys. The bad news was that Merlin had confirmed my earlier suspicion that Emrys had been poisoned. The good news was that Emrys would be okay. And the best news of all—and Merlin actually *said* this!— was that "Emrys would be okay, thanks to Cabal's quick thinking." Merlin had actually given *me* the credit! Thanks,

Merlin, I really appreciate that! But the truth is, it wasn't any big deal. After all, for some of us, performing noble deeds is something that just comes naturally.

III   The Trial of the Stone

The area around the huge black stone in the cathedral square had been entirely roped off, and it was a good thing, for just about everybody in London had come to watch the trial of the stone. We'd been smart to get an early start; otherwise we wouldn't've been able to see a blessed thing. Now we were sitting right against the rope with a view that couldn't be beat.

Several armed guards stood in the roped-off area. Some were stationed just inside the rope and others were positioned at the four corners of the huge stone. Every hour a new set of guards came to replace those who'd been standing there. We'd already seen two changings of the guard since we'd arrived.

It shouldn't be much longer now, though, because the service in the cathedral had been going on for hours. When it was over, that's when the fun would start. Emrys wasn't feeling up to much of anything yet, so Davi was our only companion. Kei had wanted to stay with us too, but the very idea of him missing the Christmas service had really irked Sir Ector. He had stern words for Kei just for thinking such a thing.

Behind the guards were the sword, the anvil, and the stone—the stone with those words carved right into it. I'm sure I don't need to remind you what they said. Even Lupus didn't need reminding. And today he wasn't even interested in pigeon chasing; because what we were going to see *today* was a once in a lifetime thing—once in a lifetime if you were lucky.

At long last, folks began filing out of the cathedral. The most important ones were allowed to stand inside the roped-off area—rank has its privilege, you know—and the lesser nobles smooshed everyone back a bit to make room for themselves. Davi and Lupus and I snuggled down beneath the rope so we could keep our clear view of the stone. When Kei and Hervey and Arthur spotted us, they came over and squeezed in, which caused some grumbling from the folks behind us.

Bishop Baldwin was in charge of things. Standing beside him was a decrepit old fellow who turned out to be the Archbishop of Canterbury, the holiest man in Britain. Also with them were Queen Igraine and old King Uther's advisors, Sir Ulfin, Sir Brastias, and Sir Jordan. I looked all over that huge crowd, trying to find the face of a person I was certain would be there. But I searched in vain—for Merlin the Wizard was nowhere to be seen.

I spotted Taliesin the Bard; and I recognized Sir Sagramore, the young knight who defeated Kei in the tournament; and I saw Sir Tristrem, the nephew of King Mark of Cornwall; and there was Rosalette, who was so fond of

Kei; and of course Sir Bedivere, Sir Lucan, and Sir Griflet. And for the briefest moment I even caught sight of my most hated enemy, the rat-faced man! Drat it, his dunking in the River Thames hadn't finished him off after all! But for the life of me I couldn't find Merlin.

When all the nobles were arranged in their positions, the Bishop of London leaped up onto the stone and raised his arms for silence.

"As most of you know, in late September on Michaelmas Eve I had a wondrous dream, a dream of revelation. I saw a sword and a stone. I saw *exactly* what you see now. I was told in my vision that we must use this sword and stone to conduct a test of virtue. That test will reveal our new King.

"As the words carved in this stone tell us, only one person will be able to pull the sword from the stone—the true-born King of Britain. Many of you will be invited to make the attempt, yet only one of you will succeed. This is the trial of the stone. When it is over, Britain will have her King.

"Who this person is I do not know, for the new King's identity wasn't revealed to me. But I truly believe that the person who succeeds in pulling the sword from the stone will be the rightful King. And I shall swear my allegiance to that person, who*ever* it is. Now—let us prepare for the trial of the stone!

"It is right and proper that the trial should begin with Britain's highest nobles. Therefore, I invite the lesser kings to step forward now and assay the stone. Any of you wishing to assay the stone should come forward now."

For a moment, no one moved. And then at almost the same time King Lot of Lothian and King Uriens of Gore stepped out from the crowd. King Nentres, curiously enough, *didn't*. And when people saw that King Nentres stood right where he was, glances were exchanged and eyebrows raised.

"My money's on King Lot," whispered Hervey. "He's three times as strong as those other blokes."

"Not a chance," Kei replied. "Lot may be strong, but Nentres is far cleverer. My money's on Nentres. I tell you, that fellow's up to something. He's got too many tricks up his sleeves for the likes of Lot."

The Bishop raised his arms for silence. Then he signaled for King Lot of Lothian to approach the stone. As Lot moved forward, a big cheer went up from his supporters. One voice stood out in that cheer, the voice of a young boy who was shouting encouragement for all he was worth. I looked over and saw that it was Gawain, the boy who'd waved so cheerily to me and Lupus yesterday.

Young Gawain appeared to be a good-hearted lad and a loyal son. But as much as I found myself liking the boy, my feelings toward his father were just the opposite. Perhaps young Gawain was as fine a lad as he appeared; but I *detested* his father, and that's flat. I'm sorry, young Gawain, I thought to myself, but I hope your father falls right on his face!

King Lot stepped onto the smaller stone that rested against the huge black one. His hand reached toward the hilt of the sword and gripped it firmly. Slowly he began exerting pressure on the sword, trying to draw it free from the anvil and stone. But the sword wasn't budging. Then Lot put all his strength into the attempt; and when he did, the huge black stone actually trembled at the force of the man's effort—yet the sword remained securely within the stone. Finally, King Lot placed his left leg against the huge stone to brace himself, put both hands on the hilt of the sword, and then tugged for all he was worth. But it was no soap. The sword didn't move, not even the teensiest bit.

King Lot knew when he was licked. He stepped down from the stone and looked directly at his silent supporters. He ran the back of his hand across his sweaty forehead and breathed out a big breath. He must've been embarrassed by his failure, but you couldn't tell it by looking at him. He summoned up a little grin, and then tilting his head to one side, he shrugged his shoulders and raised his hands with his palms turned outward. It was as if he were saying, "I gave it my all—what more can a fella do?" King Lot's modest gesture in the face of defeat brought cheers from his loyal supporters. The loudest was from the boy called Gawain.

King Uriens was the next to try. Although he was a large man, he wasn't as impressive as King Lot. In fact, many folks considered this to be more a test of Morgan le Fay's abilities than her husband's. People were guessing that if King Uriens succeeded, Morgan would've had a lot to do with it.

It was right at that moment that I finally caught a glimpse of Merlin. I *knew* he must be around here somewhere, the sly dog, and I was relieved to discover he was. Merlin wasn't among the crowd, he was standing in a window on the upper floor of a building overlooking the square. It was only because a flash of light had reflected off something in his hand that I saw him at all. Merlin was behind a curtain, just barely peeking out. But as usual he was right in the middle of things, in his own strange way.

When King Uriens stepped up to the stone and began tugging on the sword, that was when my eyes were drawn to the face of Morgan le Fay. And guess what? She wasn't even watching! Her eyes were closed, and her face wore a look of intense concentration. I had no idea what the woman was up to, but she was definitely up to *something*!

Whatever it was, it must not have worked, for Uriens failed to pull the sword from the stone. When he stepped away from the stone in defeat, Morgan looked tired and worn. At that moment she opened her eyes and looked right at the window where I'd last seen Merlin. And then Morgan's look of weariness became a look of burning rage. It wasn't her husband she was angry at. It was Merlin the Wizard.

After the unsuccessful attempts of King Lot and King Uriens, Bishop Baldwin invited other high-ranking nobles to come forward. King Nentres of Garlot wasn't among them, for the man remained steadfast in his refusal to try. But quite a few others swallowed their pride and made the attempt, futile though it was. All in all, the folks in the crowd acted respectful toward the high nobles who tried and failed. The only one who received scorn for his efforts was King Mark of Cornwall. King Mark stood up there pulling on the sword until he was red in the face. And then someone shouted out, "Don't bust a gut, Markie old boy!" That opened the door for a lot of wisecracks and catcalls. Needless to say, it wasn't a good day for King Mark.

King Uther's advisors were also asked to try. Each of them did, and each of them failed. King Leodegrance, Gwinevere's father, came up and gave it a try, and he too failed. Many a duke and many an earl and many an illustrious knight, including Sir Lucan, Sir Bedivere, and Sir Griflet, all tried, and all failed.

To tell you the truth, this day we'd had such high hopes for was turning into a big disappointment. As far as anyone could tell, there was no new High King in sight.

Every day that week the trial of the stone continued. Some of the people who'd already tried came up and tried again, but always with the same result. And other folks came hurrying to London to have a go at it, but none of them succeeded. At last even some of the lesser knights gave it a try, including Sir Ector and Sir Rhys, but of course none of them succeeded either. And all this time, King Nentres of Garlot kept on refusing to try. A lot of people were saying that King Nentres was surely the one person who could do it, if only he would try.

The Bishop of London kept the stone under close guard all that week. But that began to seem pretty pointless since it was obvious that the only person who could steal the sword would be Britain's true-born king! Believe me, people were beginning to wonder if the trial of the stone was ever going to amount to anything. Interest in the trial of the stone began to wane, and on New Year's Eve Day, the seventh day of the trial, almost no one came to attempt to pull the sword from the stone, and only a handful came to watch.

IV   An Irresistible Urge

On New Year's Day, people had something other than the trial of the stone to think about, for this was the day of the most important tournament of the whole winter. All of Britain's top knights would be there, and so would the most daring of the upstart knights—though many of Britain's fledgling knights weren't *that* daring. Kei was dead-set on being in it, and although Sir Ector wasn't sure about the wisdom of that, he finally agreed to let Kei have a go at it.

Emrys was still recovering, so Davi filled in as his squire. Lupus had to stay behind, supposedly to keep Emrys company, but really because he might get over-excited and embarrass us. Hervey and Arthur and me, along with Sir Ector and Sir Rhys, would be Kei's loyal fans and supporters.

The tournament was being held in a large open field near the Church of St. Martin. And just as earlier in the week everyone had flocked to St. Paul's to see the trial of the stone, now everyone flocked to the tournament field to see Britain's finest knights display their prowess.

We arrived at the tournament grounds with plenty of time to spare, and found the colorful tents off to one side reserved for the unestablished knights. Then Davi started laying out Kei's equipment, readying all the things he'd need for the combat. And that was when disaster struck.

"Hey, Davi," said Kei in an alarmed voice, "where's Invincible?"

"Invincible, me-lord? Why, it'll be just there in thy scabbard; just where ya put it last even, me-lord."

"No, no, Davi, *that* isn't Invincible! That's just my old practice sword. I can't use *that*! Where's Invincible? You *did* bring it along with the rest of my armor, didn't you?"

"Me-lord," said Davi, his hands beginning to tremble, "it does-na seem ta be here. It hain't with the rest of the harmor. Be ya certain ya hain't got it yourself somewheres?"

I could see that Kei, at this unexpected turn of events, was about to fly into one of his terrible rages. Fortunately, at that moment Arthur came to Davi's rescue.

"Kei," said Arthur, "there's still plenty of time to get your sword. I'll take Tawnyfoot and go fetch it. I should be back in half an hour, long before they'll call you out. You and Davi go ahead with your arming, and I'll be back by the time you've finished."

"That's the lad," said Sir Ector, clapping Arthur on the shoulder. "Be quick as you can. I'll stay here and lend a hand."

Not wanting to waste a second, Arthur and Tawnyfoot and I went zooming off on our errand. But I have to tell you, I was glad to be out of there. Until we'd gotten back with Kei's sword, Sir Ector wouldn't have an easy time of it coping with Kei.

By then we'd been in London nearly two weeks, and Arthur now knew the city like the back of his hand. He chose the quickest route, one that avoided the busier streets and took us down lesser ones on which we could really make some tracks. The route he chose led through the square in front of St. Paul's Cathedral. And as we were clattering across the square—that was when I was hit by an uncontrollable urge.

Now, I hope you realize that I'm not a dog who gets many uncontrollable urges. I get plenty of urges, sure, but most of them are controllable, even if I don't always choose to control them. But it's really unusual for me to experience a truly irresistible urge. This time I did—and I'm not just making that up. *This* time it was as if some force outside of myself had taken control of me for its own purposes.

As we were clattering across St. Paul's square, all of a sudden a crazy idea popped into my head—why not try to get the sword that was right here, the one that was sticking out of the stone? Then we wouldn't have to go all the way back to the Mermaid Inn. No one seemed to care about it anymore, and there weren't any guards to stop us. If it worked, we'd've spared Kei fifteen minutes of agony, and we'd've gotten him a better sword in the bargain.

Of course, if I'd had my wits about me, I would have realized that such an idea was utterly ridiculous. But because of the uncontrollable urge that'd taken possession of me, I didn't have my wits about me.

"Arthur!" I barked as loud as I could. "Hold on, Arthur! I've just had a fantastic idea!"

Arthur had no idea what I was getting hot and bothered about, but he certainly knew that I was worked up about something. He pulled back on Tawnyfoot's reins and swung her around to find out what kind of scrape his dog was getting into now. When he saw me charging toward the huge black stone, he shouted at me to stop. But there was no possibility of that. I was obsessed by this idea that had forced its way into my little dog brain.

"Cabal! *Stop* Cabal! What in blazes are you doing!" Arthur kept on shouting stuff like that, but it didn't do a bit of good. It wasn't that I wanted to be disobedient. I just couldn't help myself. Everything that was happening was beyond my control.

I jumped onto the smaller stone beside the huge one. I stretched my forepaws as high as they'd go, placing them on the anvil. I stretched out my head and neck as far as I could, and then I clamped my jaws around the hilt of the sword in the stone.

Holy Jerusalem, did I get the shock of my young life! As soon as my teeth were gripping the sword, a terrible thing happened. A great surge of energy crackled all through my body, and I was tingling from my nose to my toes. It was *horrible*. It felt like I'd been struck by lightning! And the terrible tingling sensation wasn't even the worst part. The worst part was that I was *stuck* to the bloomin' thing! Try as I did, I couldn't let go of that accursed sword. And all the while, that terrible current kept coursing right through my body! I would have let out the howl of my life, if only I could've opened my mouth to howl.

But before you could say Joseph of Arimathea, help was on the way. One moment Arthur was sitting on Tawnyfoot and the next he was up by my side, reaching for the sword. Arthur grabbed ahold of the sword and began wiggling it, trying to get me free. And as soon as Arthur's hands were on the sword, the terrible tingling went away and I could finally let go of the sword—or rather, *it* could finally let go of *me*!

I was free at last—and so was the sword. Arthur's wiggling had caused it to slide right out of the stone.

I felt weird and wobbly-legged, but my goodness, was it ever good to be free. I tried to shout, "way to go, master, way to go," but all I could produce were a few feeble barks.

Then the reality of the situation hit us. *The sword was out of the stone*! Arthur had just done what nobody else could do. My master Arthur had pulled the sword *out of the stone*!

Arthur looked as stunned as I felt. And his first impulse was to put the sword back in again. "No, no!" I barked frantically, finally getting my full-bodied bark back. "Let's take it to Kei! That was the whole *point* of this crazy ordeal!"

I guess Arthur must've agreed. Because after reflecting on the situation a moment, he shoved the sword through his belt and climbed up on Tawnyfoot. "C'mon, Cabal," he said in a funny-sounding voice, "let's get back to the tournament."

Kei was standing by the flap of the tent as we rushed up. His fingernails would have been bitten clean off if he hadn't been wearing steel gloves. Boy, was he happy to see us back so soon. Now he wouldn't even miss the opening ceremonies. Arthur slid down from Tawny, pulled the magnificent sword from his belt, and presented it to Kei.

"Sorry it isn't Invincible," Arthur said. "Under the circumstances, I didn't think you'd mind."

Kei stared at the sword as if thunderstruck. Then he threw his head back and let loose a gale of nervous laughter. "No," he managed at last, "it certainly isn't Invincible. And under the circumstances, I don't mind a bit."

Kei began swinging the sword through the air, making feints and thrusts, getting a feel for the heft and balance of the beautiful sword. But that was all there was time for, because at that point Sir Ector came out of the tent. He was eager to get Kei to the tournament field. But as things turned out, Kei never got there.

I don't think it had dawned on Kei yet just what sword Arthur had brought him. He knew it was a better sword than Invincible, but it never crossed his mind that it was the sword from the stone. But Sir Ector had to take only one look at the sword to know what it was. And when he did, the poor man's face turned pale as the winter moon.

"Oh my gracious, Kei! What are you doing with *that*? How in the world did you *get* it?"

A moment before, Kei had been delighting in his new weapon. Now he knew he was about to be in hot water. He did some very quick thinking, trying to find a way out of the jam he was in. But for once it was Arthur who spoke first. "It's the sword from the stone, father. We thought Kei could use it instead of Invincible."

"Kei," said Sir Ector, looking at his son very seriously. "Did *you* pull the sword from the stone?"

Kei looked down at his feet for a moment, and then he glanced over at Arthur. And then he said in a clear firm voice, "That's right, father, just a few minutes ago. I pulled the sword right out of the stone. It really wasn't so difficult, father."

Now it was poor Sir Ector's turn to look thunderstruck. I don't believe he thought it was possible that Kei could have done this; and yet there was the sword, right in Kei's hand. He looked at Arthur and then he looked at Kei. The boys stood there nervously, neither of them saying a word.

Finally Sir Ector let out a huge sigh. "Well, lads, there's nothing else for it but to go back to the cathedral and see if you can do it again. Get your horses and let's be on our way."

As they were doing that, one of the young knights standing nearby glanced over and noticed the sword Kei was holding. "Hey," he shouted, "that's the sword from the stone, isn't it? That really looks like the sword from the stone!"

And that was all it took. People came rushing over to see, and then a hue and cry was raised all over the tournament grounds and in the grandstand—"A young knight's got the sword from the stone!" "Look, everybody, someone's taken the sword from the stone!"

I guess the tournament we'd all been so excited about would just have to wait. Because as our little group began making its way back to St. Paul's Square, a gigantic procession of folks was following along behind us. It looked as though this was going to turn into quite an event. All the important clergymen and all the highest-ranking nobles were coming along also. Soon the Bishop of London was there, and so was Queen Igraine and her advisors, and so were all the lesser kings.

Right at that moment I was very happy that I wasn't the one standing in Kei's boots. Kei, I was pretty sure, was just about to find himself in the biggest jam of his life. Because if Kei could pull the sword out of the stone, I'd eat Merlin's hat!

V   The True-Born
King of Britain

I didn't know what would happen when we reached the cathedral square. One thing I did know, though, was that I was not going to have anything to do with pulling swords out of stones. For me, once was enough. If Kei and Arthur couldn't get through this business without my help, that would be *their* problem. When it comes to swords in stones, I found myself in complete agreement with King Nentres of Garlot— the wisest course is to steer clear of the blasted things!

This time the Bishop of London didn't take charge, and Sir Ector was allowed to handle the situation in his own way. Bishop Baldwin stood off to one side with all the other high-ranking nobles. But they were taking a very keen interest in the entire proceeding. Sir Ector led Kei and Arthur right up to the stone. And then Sir Ector took the sword from Kei and slid it down through the anvil and back into the stone.

Then the sword, the anvil, and the stone seemed to be exactly the way they were on the day they'd first appeared in the cathedral square. Just to be sure, Sir Ector reached out and grabbed the sword and tugged on it; but the darn thing didn't budge a bit. Then Sir Ector stepped back from the huge stone and turned to Kei.

"Now, Kei," he said softly to his son, "I want you to show me how you got the sword."

Kei shifted nervously from one foot to the other. He didn't seem very eager to do much of anything. Everybody was watching him, and now Kei had come down with a major case of cold feet. That was when Kei's sense of honor finally got the better of him.

"Father," he said, "I *wasn't* the one who pulled the sword from the stone. It was Arthur who brought me the sword, father. I don't know how he got it." Then Kei began studying his toes.

Sir Ector placed his hand gently on Kei's shoulder. To my surprise, he didn't seem angry. In fact, he looked relieved—relieved, I think, that Kei hadn't been the one who pulled the sword out of the stone, and relieved that Kei had managed to cough up the truth.

Then Sir Ector turned to Arthur. Arthur stood there tall and silent, as if to say, whatever's going to happen is going to happen. I felt proud of my master. Nervous though he surely was, he wasn't shying away from whatever medicine was about to be dished out.

"Arthur," said Sir Ector. "Did *you* pull the sword from the stone?"

Arthur looked straight at Sir Ector. The gaze of the older man met the gaze of the younger man, and neither of them looked away. "Father," said Arthur, "I guess I did. But it happened in a strange way. I wasn't even trying to get the sword. I was just trying to help Cabal."

I don't think Arthur's explanation made a whole lot of sense to Sir Ector just then, and to tell you the truth, there was no reason why it should have. But Sir Ector didn't ask Arthur to do any more explaining. He passed right over the weirdness of Arthur's remarks and moved on to more important matters.

"Arthur, I would like to see if you can pull the sword out of the stone again."

Arthur wasn't any more eager to attempt this than Kei had been. But under the circumstances, he didn't have a lot of choice. It was what his father wanted him to do, and it was what everyone watching expected him to do. So Arthur stepped over to the stone, climbed up onto the smaller one, and reached out for the sword. He grasped the hilt in his right hand, and then very slowly and gently he pulled the sword straight out of the stone. A huge gasp was emitted from a multitude of mouths. I don't think anyone there had expected Arthur to be able to do it. But he had.

At that point Bishop Baldwin spoke up. "Young man," he said, "I would like you to put the sword back into the stone. Would you do that for me, please?" A rather stunned-looking Arthur did what the bishop wanted. He slid the sword right back where it had been.

Then the bishop asked Kei to try to pull it out. Kei was still feeling pretty nervous about the whole business, but of course he did what the bishop asked him to. He gripped the sword firmly and gave it a good tug. Nothing happened. Then he pulled as hard as he could, but he couldn't remove it.

"Sir Bedivere," said the bishop. "I would be grateful if you would try to remove the sword from the stone."

"Of course, your grace," said Sir Bedivere. And he came up obligingly and tried to pull out the sword. But he had no more success than Kei.

"Young man," said the bishop to Arthur, "I would like you to try once more to remove the sword from the stone." So yet again Arthur did what he was asked to do, and yet again he drew the sword straight out of the stone.

"Young man," said the bishop to Arthur, "am I correct in assuming that this knight is your father?" The bishop, of course, was referring to Sir Ector.

"Yes, your grace, he *is* my father," Arthur replied.

And that was the moment when a woman said very clearly, "*No*, your grace, with all due respect, Sir Ector *isn't* his father."

Out from the crowd stepped Queen Igraine, followed by Uther Pendragon's advisors Sir Ulfin, Sir Brastias, and Sir Jordan.

"If it pleases your grace," the queen said, "I think the time has come to reveal the true identity of this young man named Arthur." Well, as you can imagine, Queen Igraine's words really pricked up the ears of the folks in that crowd!

"This young man," the queen went on, "contrary to what he has always thought, is not the son of the good knight Sir Ector. Nor is he the brother of the young knight Sir Kei.

Your grace, this young man is the only son of King Uther Pendragon." Hearing *this*, the crowd gave out another gasp, and this one was even bigger than the earlier one.

"*That can't be true!*" a man shouted out. "Uther Pendragon died without offspring! Uther Pendragon had *no* sons!" It won't surprise you to learn that the one who was challenging the queen was King Lot of Lothian.

"My dear Lot," said the queen rather coldly, "I think perhaps *I* would know better than you whether or not King Uther had any children. And I assure you, this young man is the King's son. I should know, because I am his *mother*."

Right on cue, the crowd gave another gasp. And me and a whole lot of others started looking back and forth between Arthur and the queen, the queen and Arthur. My heart went out to poor Arthur, who stood there looking distinctly like a dazed quail. The poor lad was stunned by these startling revelations. But the queen had a very warm smile for Arthur, a smile that shone on her lips and in her eyes—her eyes that looked so much like Arthur's eyes. Anyone there could see how much Arthur and Igraine looked like each other. Why, I'd noticed it the first time I'd seen the woman!

But Lot wasn't through raising objections. "How do we know this is true?" he shouted. "What proof can you offer that this beardless youth is really Uther's son? I say this is a trick! I say this young whelp shall *never* be king!"

"Well, I say he *shall!*" came the voice of another man. This time the speaker was King Nentres of Garlot; and as soon as folks identified the speaker, another gasp arose from the crowd.

"There is no reason for us to doubt the words of the queen," King Nentres declared. "I'm sure Sir Ulfin and the others will support what she has said. And I also believe in the truth of the Bishop's dream and in the veracity of the stone. This lad has pulled the sword from the stone. That's all the proof any of us should need!"

"I completely agree." Now joining the rancorous consultation was the voice of another woman, and heads were jerked quickly in her direction to see who it was. It was Morgan le Fay.

"My mother has told you the truth," Morgan said. "This young man, whom I willingly accept as my own true brother, is the one that we must acknowledge as our liege lord and king." And having said that, she went down to her knees before Arthur.

And when she did, nearly everyone else followed her example, except for King Lot and a few of his most loyal followers. But to my surprise, the young boy named Gawain, a lad who'd already won me over as a friend, went down to his knees also. And I saw him gazing at Arthur with a look of awe on his face.

By this time Arthur had begun to look a little less dazed, but now he'd begun to look terribly embarrassed. How would *you* feel if you'd been going along happily in your life, thinking that you're just an ordinary sort of bloke, when all of a sudden everybody bows down to you and starts calling you their liege lord? It might give you a little pause, too.

"Please, father," said Arthur, addressing his words to Sir Ector, and sounding a little desperate. "Please rise up, father." Arthur reached down and took ahold of Sir Ector's shoulders and gently helped him to his feet. Then Sir Ector gazed upon this young man whom he'd raised as his son, this young man whom he loved like a son.

"Arthur," said Sir Ector, "you must think of me no longer as your father. I am now no more than one of your ordinary vassals. I have loved you, Arthur, like my own flesh and blood, and I always will. But you can no longer think of me as your father. The time has come, as I knew it would, when you must set about doing all you can for Britain. But if there is ever anything I can do for you, you know that I will." As the good Sir Ector was saying these words, there were tears in the corners of his eyes. And there were tears in Arthur's eyes, too.

"You *are* my father," Arthur replied, sounding as if his heart might break. "You will *always* be my father. Since the queen has said that I am the son of King Uther Pendragon, I suppose it must be so. But *you* will always be my father. You have never denied me the love a father should give his son, and I will never deny you the love a son should give his father."

Sir Ector put his arms around Arthur and hugged him. And then he released his hold on Arthur and stepped back, holding the young man at arm's length.

"I do have one request, Arthur," said Sir Ector. "I hope you will find a place in your royal court for Kei. I hope you will always keep Kei with you."

"Father," said Arthur, "Kei is my brother. And as long as he wishes to be with me, he will always have a place of the highest honor. Once Kei saved my life, and I know that he would never hesitate to do it again. But," said Arthur with a grin, "I don't think you need to worry too much about Kei. Kei's pretty good at taking care of himself."

"*Enough* of this nonsense!" came the booming voice of King Lot, who was obviously fed up with all this sentimental gush. "I say the boy is a fraud! And unless it can be proved that Uther really was his father, I will never acknowledge him as my liege lord. Unless it can be *proved*, I will make war upon anyone who sides with this pathetic upstart crow!"

"What more proof do you *want*?" Sir Ulfin shot back at King Lot. "He's pulled the sword from the stone, he's been accepted by the bishop and all the other kings, and he's been acknowledged by the queen herself. He's been accepted by everyone here but *you*!"

"But *Uther* never acknowledged him! If Uther had a son, he would never have kept it a secret, he would have thrown the boy in our faces. Uther had *no children*! Uther wasn't even *able* to have children! A real king is known by the progeny he produces." And King Lot made a sweeping motion above the heads of his sons. "Where is Uther's acknowledgment of this boy? I say this boy is a nobody, and we are fools if we don't reject him now!"

Well, I had had more than my fill of King Lot's windy talk. Now it was time for action. I rushed up to Arthur and started tugging at the little pouch that was tied to his belt under his cloak. He'd been wearing it since Merlin had had his little chat with Arthur and me when we'd first come to London. For a moment, Arthur didn't realize what I was doing, the silly goose, but then he did.

Arthur reached for the pouch and pulled it loose from his belt. He opened it and removed a piece of dark red cloth. Then he unfolded the cloth. In the palm of his hand Arthur now held the silver dragon brooch he'd been given a long time ago by King Uther Pendragon, back in our little chamber in the Red Castle.

Arthur studied the brooch for a moment, and then holding it between his thumb and first two fingers, he lifted it high above his head. As soon as everyone caught sight of it, there was yet another gasp from the crowd, for everyone recognized the Pendragon emblem that King Uther had always worn. Arthur fastened the brooch to his cloak. And that beautiful dragon, with its fiery red eye, sparkled magnificently in the bright sunshine.

My master Arthur stood there in the cathedral square, tall and silent. To my way of thinking, young though he was, Arthur looked every inch a king. And now, with the visual proof of his connection to King Uther staring them right in the face, everyone dropped down to their knees once again. And this time, so did King Lot of Lothian.

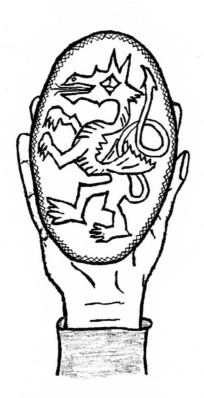

VI   A Fly in the Ointment

O h, how I wished Merlin could've been there to share that moment. How proud the old duffer would've been, for it seemed as if everyone in the world were kneeling before Arthur. And then somehow I knew that he *was* there—I could feel it in my bones. Merlin was there all right, and he was seeing exactly what I was seeing. "Merlin, you sly dog," I shouted inside my head, "where the dickens are you?"

I whirled myself about looking this way and that, checking every doorway, window, and rooftop. Finally I spotted the old geezer in a window overlooking the square. As usual, he was peeping out from behind a curtain.

"Merlin," I shouted inside my head, not knowing if he could hear me, "did you ever imagine that you'd see such a sight? Did you ever imagine that such things could happen?"

To my great surprise, a voice came thundering back inside my head, "As a matter of fact, my dear Cabal, I *did* imagine that such things could happen!"

Before I could stop and consider *this* peculiar development—for Merlin had spoken to me *inside* my own head!—something else happened that diverted my attention. For right at that moment I sensed movement down below Merlin's window, and I couldn't help zeroing in on it. It's a good thing I did, for by stretching my neck and looking out over the heads of those folks who were down on their knees, I saw a man standing in a doorway, a man who was holding a crossbow. It was none other than my most hated enemy, *the rat-faced man*!

The square was so silent you could've heard a feather drop. Everyone was on their knees, waiting for Arthur to do something; and Arthur, being a bit new to all this, wasn't sure what to do. And no one there had noticed the rat-faced man— no one but me.

Then the silence of St. Paul's square was shattered by the yelping and barking of a frantic dog. "It's the rat-faced man, Merlin," I shouted with all my might, "it's the stinking rat-faced man!"

Now the rat-faced man had brought the stock of the crossbow up against his cheek. He was holding it steady, sighting along the top; and then he released the catch. An arrow came leaping from the bow, flying straight and true, heading right for Arthur. At that point there was only one thing to do, and I was the only one who could do it. I hurled myself forward, directly into the path of the arrow.

For a fraction of a second it was dog vs. arrow—and I knew how *that* was likely to turn out! And then *poof*, the arrow was gone. One moment it was there and then it was gone. And hanging in the air where I'd last seen it was a little wisp of smoke.

"*Thank you, Merlin!*" I yelped with joy. How delicious it was to be alive and kicking!

But it must've seemed a strange sight to all those folks gathered there—first, a wild-eyed dog starts barking his fool head off, and then he's chasing phantoms in the air right in front of Arthur! But I couldn't be bothered with folks' opinions just then, for there was a crucial piece of business that required my attention. The time had come to take care of that rat-faced man—once and for all.

I sprinted across the square past a lot of wide-eyed, opened-mouth folks. The rat-faced man, seeing me charging like a bee-stung bull, tossed down his crossbow and retreated into the building. As I flew through the doorway, I could hear his footsteps ascending the stairs. I shot up those stairs like a hound after its quarry, and the rat-faced man, knowing I was closing in, dashed into a room and tried to close the door on me. But I wedged myself through before he could. Then he fled across the room and out through a pair of doors that opened onto a balcony. Now the blighter was *trapped*— trapped like a stinking rat! But he whirled around with a snarl; and with his back against the railing, he pulled out a knife.

Too late! I snapped, hurling myself forward with all the power I could muster. I smashed into his chest, and his knife spun away in the air. And then so did the rat-faced man and me—for the railing he'd been leaning against had given way.

I did a couple of flips and then came down hard on the cobblestones of St. Paul's square. I lay there stunned, the air knocked out of me. For a flickering moment I was back at the Red Castle where some barmy horse had just bashed me a good one.

But as my senses began to clear, I saw folks hovering over me, and one of them, thank goodness, was Arthur. Then I realized that folks were hovering over the rat-face man, too, including Sir Bedivere and Sir Griflet. Those fellows didn't hesitate to grab the slimy varlet and jerk him to his feet. Arthur's gentle touch was doing wonders for me, and in the next moment I was up on my feet.

A wide circle had formed around us, and all those folks were gawking and gaping, wondering what in the world had been going on.

"It's time for you to provide some answers," Arthur said to the rat-faced man. "If you value your life, you'd better be speaking up. Now, who are you, and who's behind all these little pranks of yours?"

When the rat-faced man didn't say anything, Sir Griflet gave him a sharp elbow to the ribs. "What was *that*?" said Sir Griflet. "I couldn't quite make that out."

"I dint say nowt," wheezed the rat-face man. "And I ain't goin' ta say nowt."

Without beating around the bush Arthur came right out and said what most of us were thinking. "You've been working for King Lot, haven't you. Admit it, *he's* the one who's put you up to all of this."

"My *liege* lord!" shouted King Lot, sounding truly shocked at Arthur's words. "I know *nothing* of this man! I promise you, I've never even *seen* him before! I won't deny that I've wanted to be High King, but I would *never* stoop to foul play!"

His words sounded so sincere and his face looked so honest that I actually found myself believing the guy! And so, I think, did Arthur. But if the rat-faced man wasn't working for Lot, as I'd been assuming all along, then who the devil *was* he working for? Morgan le Fay? Somehow, I didn't think so.

Then my eyes fell on King Nentres of Garlot. He was standing there quietly with just a hint of a smile on his face, looking like a sleek black cat. I remembered what Kei had said about him—that he had a lot of tricks up his well-furred sleeves. That's when I was pretty sure who the rat-faced man was *really* working for. King Nentres, I said to myself, is a fellow who's going to need some very close watching. There may be *more* rat-faced guys lurking out there—rats working for a sleek black cat! My days of being Arthur's loyal guardian, I realized, were far from over.

"We've got a nice little cell in the Tower that should suit this fellow just fine, my liege," said Sir Griflet. "And if it's all right with you, we'll take him there now and see if we can't pry the truth out of him. We've got some special implements there that always seem to do the trick."

Arthur stared at Sir Griflet for a moment, a little taken aback by what the fellow was suggesting. "Well, okay," he finally agreed, "you can take him to the Tower. But I want you to treat him well. I'll be talking to him myself in a few days, and when I do, I expect to find him in a fit condition."

"Indeed, my liege," replied Sir Griflet with a small bow of his head. "We'll see that he's properly taken care of."

Finally Arthur looked down at me. Flashing me a big happy grin, he reached down and tousled the fur on the back of my neck. "You're quite a fellow, Cabal," he said softly, "quite a fellow." For once my master had found just the right words for the occasion.

VII The Times,

They are a-Changin'

That evening we went back to the Mermaid Inn for the last time. My goodness, what a difference a day makes! Sir Lucan, Sir Griflet, and Sir Bedivere went along with us. They were going to be Arthur's constant companions from now on. Other folks came along too, to help us get ready to move to King Uther's royal palace outside the city near a place called Westminster. But these folks really didn't have a whole lot to do, because we had traveled pretty light on our journey from the Red Castle.

There was surprisingly little celebrating that night. I think everyone was still rather stunned by the day's incredible events. It was going to take a while for all of this to sink in and for us to adjust to this sudden change in our fortunes. Arthur, however, after his initial shock and dismay, had become surprisingly calm about everything. I had the impression that Arthur was turning a whole lot of things over very carefully in his mind.

Of course we had a stream of visitors stopping by the inn, but Sir Bedivere and Sir Lucan let only a select few in to see us. Heading the list was Gwinevere and her father King

Leodegrance. Believe me, that young woman was beside herself with delight. And now that our circumstances had been so dramatically altered, Arthur seemed much shyer around Gwinevere than he'd been before. When she came over to him and gave him a hug and a tender little kiss on the cheek, Arthur blushed like I'd never seen before.

Taliesin the Bard was allowed in, too, and despite the fact that our fortunes had taken this turn for the better, good old Taliesin seemed just the same as ever. He offered his services to the new young king, and they were eagerly accepted. Arthur told Taliesin he would be welcomed at his court any time he chose to come, and he hoped it would be often. Then Taliesin sat off to one side and played some gentle little tunes on his harp.

Arthur spent much of the evening visiting with his mother Queen Igraine, who'd been accompanied to the Mermaid Inn by Sir Ulfin. The three of them sat together chatting quietly for quite some time, with the queen doing most of the talking, and Arthur just lapping up her words like a big-eyed pup. But contrary to what you might expect, I really didn't overhear much of their conversation. I was more interested just then in sitting close to Taliesin and listening to his soft little melodies. I have to admit it, since that night long ago in the Forest of Dean when we'd first met Taliesin, I'd developed quite a fondness for the sounds of his little Welsh harp.

Later that evening Merlin finally showed up, and goodness, did he ever look exhausted. He looked like a fellow who was in desperate need of a long and lazy holiday. "Merlin," I said inside my head, "you've been working too hard, old-timer." Merlin turned his head and gave me quite a stare. And then, just as I was beginning to get a little nervous, he flashed me the biggest smile that I'd ever seen on his withered old face.

"Cabal," he said, "I think you may be right."

The folks around us who overheard Merlin talking to me like that just looked at one another and shook their heads as if to say, that Merlin is one strange fellow. Of course, they didn't know that Merlin and I were in the midst of a conversation, so who could blame them?

Merlin spoke quietly to Sir Ector, and then he spoke to Kei. At last he settled down in a chair right next to Arthur and me. As the other folks went on with their various businesses, the three of us just sat there in silence. Then Merlin reached over with his sour-apple hands and began rubbing me behind my ears.

"Arthur," Merlin said. "You know, you picked out a pretty good dog for yourself. I'll bet Tom kennelman wishes he still had this dog of yours. And Arthur, one of the things I like best about this gentle grass-eating dog is the way he controls the powerful urges he sometimes gets. Of course, he doesn't *always* manage to control them, does he." Then Merlin's eyes met mine and he gave me a great big wink.

Arthur started petting me too, and between the two of them they were ruffling my feathers pretty good. But I think you know that I loved every second of it.

But as I sat there being manhandled by my two best friends in the world, a thought came strolling into my little dog brain. That irresistable urge that I'd had—the one that had gotten me into such a jam in St. Paul's Square—could old Merlin have had something to do with that? Was that what he was getting at when he said I didn't *always* manage to control my urges?

As I sat there thinking about this, I realized that Merlin and Arthur and I make a pretty good team. I realized that all the amazing things which had come to pass couldn't have happened without the three of us working together. Well, I guess one just has to face the facts sometimes. We really do make a pretty good team, Arthur and Merlin and me.

Author's Note

Some of the earliest medieval works about King Arthur say that he had a remarkable dog named Cabal or Cavall. In one tale found in the early Welsh work *The Mabinogion* Arthur and Cabal chase a demonic boar named Twrch Trwyth. In an even earlier work there is a reference to a huge footprint left by Cabal high up on a mountaintop in Wales during the same famous hunt for the monstrous boar. Later medieval works have little to say about Arthur's dog, but in more recent times writers have once again begun to include Cabal in stories relating the tale of Arthur.

The name Cabal comes from an ancient European word meaning "horse," and the root of that word still can be seen in such words as *chivalry* and *cavalier* and in the Spanish words *caballo* and *caballero*. Also remaining in English is the word *cob*, a term for a sturdy, short-legged work horse. It seems likely that Arthur's dog was named Cabal because he was a large and powerful animal who perhaps bore some resemblance to a small horse.

Medieval tellers of the story of Arthur create a world of fantasy and the imagination, but it is also a world that is somewhat similar to the world in which they lived, the world of the High European Middle Ages, which lasted from the 12th Century to the 15th Century. This was the great age of medieval castles and cathedrals. The actual figure upon whom the Arthur legends is based would have lived much earlier, probably in the late 5th or early 6th Centuries, a time known as the British Dark Ages. The real Arthur, assuming that such a person actually existed, probably wouldn't have been very much like the figure portrayed in the great medieval versions of the story. But it is the Arthur of Geoffrey of Monmouth and Chretien de Troyes and Thomas Malory with whom we are familiar, and it is from those great medieval renditions of the story that I have drawn.